K

17

# More Tales of the Wild West

**OTHER SAGEBRUSH LARGE PRINT WESTERNS BY**
# MAX BRAND

---

The Abandoned Outlaw: A Western Trio
A Circle Ⓥ Western

The City in the Sky
A Circle Ⓥ Western

Farewell Thunder Moon

Fugitives' Fire

The Legend of Thunder Moon

The Night Horseman

The One-Way Trail: A Western Trio
A Circle Ⓥ Western

The Quest of Lee Garrison

Safety McTee: A Western Trio
A Circle Ⓥ Western

Slumber Mountain: A Western Trio
A Circle Ⓥ Western

Soft Metal: A Western Trio
A Circle Ⓥ Western

Tales of the Wild West: Western Stories
A Circle Ⓥ Western

Thunder Moon and Red Wind

Thunder Moon and the Sky People

Two Sixes: A Western Trio
A Circle Ⓥ Western

The Untamed

# More Tales of the Wild West

## Western Stories

## MAX BRAND™

### *With a Foreword and Headnotes by*
## WILLIAM F. NOLAN

## A Circle Ⓥ Western

**Sagebrush**
**Large Print Westerns**

**Library of Congress Cataloging in Publication Data**

Cataloging-in-Publication data was not available in time for the printing of this book. Please contact us and we will mail or fax the information to you.

A **Circle Ⓥ Western** published by Thomas T. Beeler in cooperation with Golden West Literary Agency. All rights reserved.
First Edition.
*First Printing, January 1999*

**Sagebrush Large Print Westerns** are published in the United States and Canada by Thomas T. Beeler, Publisher, Post Office Box 659, Hampton Falls, New Hampshire 03844-0659. ISBN 1-57490-169-9

Published in the United Kingdom, Eire, and the Republic of South Africa by Isis Publishing Ltd, 7 Centremead, Osney Mead, Oxford OX2 0ES  England. ISBN 0-7531-6005-6

Published in Australia and New Zealand by Australian Large Print Audio & Video Pty Ltd, 17 Mohr Street, Tullamarine, Victoria, 3043, Australia. ISBN 1-88442-263-7

Manufactured in the United States of America by BookCrafters, Inc.

# ACKNOWLEDGMENTS

"A Lucky Dog" under the byline John Frederick first appeared in Street & Smith's *Western Story Magazine* (10/22/27). Copyright © 1927 by Street & Smith Publications, Inc. Copyright © renewed 1955 by Dorothy Faust. Copyright © 1999 by Jane Faust Easton and Adriana Faust Bianchi for restored material. Acknowledgment is made to Condé Nast Publications, Inc., for their co-operation.

"Inverness" first appeared under the title "Sleeper Turns Horse-Thief" by Max Brand in *Mavericks* (12/34). Copyright © 1934 by Popular Publications Inc. Copyright © renewed 1961 by Jane Faust Easton, John Frederick Faust, and Judith Faust. Copyright © 1999 by Jane Faust Easton and Adriana Faust Bianchi for restored material.

"Crazy Rhythm" by Max Brand first appeared in *Argosy* (3/2/35). Copyright © 1935 by Frank A. Munsey Company. Copyright © renewed 1962 by Jane Faust Easton, John Frederick Faust, and Judith Faust. Copyright © 1999 by Jane Faust Easton and Adriana Faust Bianchi for restored material.

"Death in Alkali Flat" first appeared under the title "Sun and Sand" by Hugh Owen in Street & Smith's *Western Story Magazine* (2/16/35). Copyright © 1935 by Street & Smith Publications, Inc. Copyright © renewed 1962 by Jane Faust Easton, John Frederick Faust, and Judith Faust. Copyright © 1999 by Jane Faust Easton and Adriana Faust Bianchi for restored material. Acknowledgment is made to Condé Nast Publications, Inc., for their co-operation.

"Blondy" first appeared under the title "Bulldog" by Max Brand in *Collier's* (2/23/24). Copyright © 1924 by P. F. Collier and Son. Copyright © renewed 1951 by Dorothy Faust. Copyright © 1999 by Jane Faust Easton and Adriana Faust Bianchi for restored material.

"A First Blooding" by Max Brand first appeared in THE NEW FRONTIER (Doubleday, 1989), edited by Joe R. Lansdale. Copyright © 1989 by Western Writers of America.

To STEPHEN KING

who appreciates the magic of Max Brand

# TABLE OF CONTENTS

# FOREWORD

Two of the six stories in the present collection originally appeared in Street & Smith's *Western Story Magazine*. A detailed look at Frederick Faust's incredible relationship with this publication and its editor, Frank Blackwell, is long overdue. No other writer in the colorful history of the pulps ever produced more wordage for a single magazine. Faust's saga with *Western Story Magazine* is the stuff of legend.

A high-level executive decision in April of 1915—when Faust was still attending the University of California at Berkeley—resulted in a new addition to the editorial staff at Street & Smith Publications in New York. Frank E. Blackwell, formerly a reporter and feature writer for the New York *Sun*, possessed a natural talent for editing. He quickly manifested this talent by taking over the publishing company's first all-mystery pulp, *Detective Story Magazine*, which made its newsstand debut in early October, 1915. By 1917, due to the magazine's solid success, it became a weekly, and gained a lasting reputation as the most popular and widely read crime publication in the world.

If such success could be achieved with mystery fiction, then what about trying the same approach with an all-Western pulp? In 1919, Street & Smith decided to scuttle their outdated *Buffalo Bill Weekly* and replace it with a new bi-weekly title, *Western Story Magazine*. Frank Blackwell was handed the editorial reins. The first issue, dated July 12, 1919, bore a heading that would typify the magazine: "Big Clean Stories of Western Life." The new pulp was an instant success;

within four months its circulation had reached three hundred thousand.

Street & Smith was anxious to turn their new magazine into a weekly, and a prolific writer as a mainstay, someone who could be counted upon to supply a sufficient amount of wordage to support weekly publication, would be a tremendous advantage. And that writer needed to have a genuine talent for the Western genre. Blackwell had been following the career of Max Brand in the Munsey pulps and was aware of Faust's close relationship with editor Robert Davis. Here was a writer who'd been selling steadily to the Frank A. Munsey magazines since 1917. In fact, he'd turned out so many stories that Munsey was now backlogged with his material. "By 1920 Bob Davis was over-bought on Faust," declared Blackwell, "and Munsey told Bob he'd have to shut off buying for six months and use up the stuff in the safe. Faust, always in need of money no matter how much he made, came to me with a story. I bought it. . . and he was mine and mine only from there on."

The firm had found its mainstay writer. A new pen name, George Owen Baxter—the first of several created for *Western Story Magazine*; the others were Peter Henry Morland, David Manning, George Challis, Hugh Owen, Evin Evan, Peter Dawson, and Martin Dexter—was attached to Faust's initial story for Blackwell, "Jerry Peyton's Notched Inheritance," a serial that began in the eighth weekly issue of *Western Story* dated November 25, 1920.

Blackwell's smug declaration that Faust was "mine and mine only" was not really true, since during his extended tenure with Street & Smith Faust also sold fiction to more than a dozen other markets, appearing in *Argosy/All-Story Weekly, Ace-High, Country Gentleman, Short Stories, Collier's, Detective Fiction Weekly, American Weekly, Argosy, Railroad Man's Magazine, Dime Western, Illustrated Love, West,* and *Adventure.* Admittedly these appearances were scattered and limited to sporadic sales. Certainly the vast bulk of Faust's writing between 1921 and 1934 was done for Blackwell and *Western Story Magazine.* (Early in this period he also wrote a handful of crime tales under the byline Nicholas Silver for *Detective Story Magazine.*) Working mainly as Brand, Baxter, John Frederick, Manning, and Morland, he produced a staggering thirteen million words of Western fiction for this one magazine, equal to almost two hundred full-length novels!

Faust quit writing for Street & Smith late in 1933, although a few more of his stories, aimed for other markets, were eventually printed there into 1938. Until Blackwell severely cut Faust's rate in the Depression years of the early 1930s—causing him to seek other markets—he was paid five cents a word. More than any other pulp writer in this penny-a-word business. At his peak, Faust could earn $5,000 for a serial he could slam out in a week on his portable typewriter. In the 1920s (when a dollar was worth twenty times what it is today), Faust was earning $75,000 a year just from *Western Story Magazine.* During 1932, when he wrote more than a million-and-a-half words for Blackwell, Faust appeared in every weekly issue, regularly under two names and, in a dozen issues that year, under *three* names, often producing more than sixty-thousand words each week.

In the back of every issue, Blackwell would announce forthcoming fiction. In 1932, one such announcement read:

Banner issue next week, folks. The first installment of a great serial by George Owen Baxter. George calls his latest "Lucky Larrabee." Dashing title that! And the story does not belie its name. Then there is a complete novel by Max Brand. His handle for the story is "Speedy's Crystal Game," and it's as fast as its name. Then. . . . the second installment of "The Golden Spurs" by David Manning. And then, folks, with next week's issue begins a serial by a new man, Evin Evan: "Montana Rides." [This odd pen name became "Evan Evans" when the serial was put into book form.] Some of the critics on this here editorial ranch have declared this yarn to be something extra. . . . She sure does move, that's one thing certain.

As Street & Smith historian Quentin Reynolds noted: "Hundreds of letters would come to the desk of editor Blackwell debating the relative merits of George Owen Baxter, Max Brand, David Manning and the 'new' writer, Evin Evan. Had anyone ever told the faithful reader that they were all one and the same man, he would have risked getting scalped. Each reader had his favorite."

In order to head off the suspicions of astute readers who might have noticed similar styles and themes in the work of Brand, Baxter, and Manning—the magazine's "big three"—Blackwell manufactured separate fake bios of each, printing them as fact in the magazine.

Brand, according to *Western Story Magazine*, was a top hand at the "Ranch Cross B, born and raised on the range." At ten, he saved the lives of his two aunts in a runaway wagon by leaping on the back of one of the team horses and pulling it to a stop. A true hero, he wrote about true heroes.

George Owen Baxter's father, "James Baxter," was described as "a wealthy ranch owner in southern California" who fell in love with a schoolteacher. They married and settled down together on his ranch, where young George learned to rope, ride, and herd cattle. In college they called George "the cowboy kid." He was a moody student, "homesick for the rolling plains, the night rides under the stars, and the rough, kindly cowboys of his father's ranch." When a telegram arrived, telling him that his father had been hurt in a stampede, George left college to return to the ranch. He was back where he belonged. The cowboy kid had come home.

David Manning was a "pampered, only child," prone to illness, with a primitive education. Restless, he left home early where he "trapped, prospected, mined a little, and roved through nearly every state in the Union." He finally ended up as a columnist on a small Western newspaper, writing about desert life. The bio ends with Manning pounding out fiction for *Western Story Magazine* on a battered typewriter deep in the wilds "breathing the air and spirit of the country, living. . . the romantic splendor of it all."

It is doubtful that Faust ever read about these fabricated Western lives, but he made it plain that his early boyhood years, when he labored from dawn to dusk on the farms and ranches of central California, had been painful and agonizing. Brand, Baxter, and Manning may have loved the "romantic splendor" of the West, but for Frederick Faust it held dark memories. The West he wrote about was a land of pure imagination, far away from the cow dung, killing weather, and unwashed cowboys of his youth.

The most amazing thing about Faust was his ability to turn out such an incredible amount of fiction each year. His manuscripts were "stacked like cordwood" along the walls of his agent's office in New York, and, when he was asked how he could write so much in so short a time, Faust would reply: "There's a giant asleep in every man. When that giant awakes, miracles can happen."

He was being too generous in attributing his own giantism to "every man." Actually, Faust was unique in producing his miracles. No other writer in history turned out more words in a given period. In all, under eleven pen names, he appeared eight hundred and thirty-three times in six hundred and twenty-one issues of *Western Story Magazine* from late 1920 into 1935. Thanks to his massive output, the magazine reached a circulation in 1922 of two million weekly readers.

Although he lived in a villa above Florence in the hills of Italy, Faust was forced to make occasional business trips to New York where he would confer with Frank Blackwell on upcoming works. Their relations were always cordial, but there was no personal warmth between them. To Blackwell, Faust was a necessary "fiction factory." To Faust, Blackwell was a steady source of income. Each needed the other.

Faust's son-in-law, novelist and biographer Robert Easton, in his ***Max Brand: The Big "Westerner"*** (1970) described the Street & Smith building at 78-79 Seventh Avenue as resembling a prison: "grim and gloomy. . . a dour square of red brick with industrial windows and a steam elevator operated by a man who looked like a trusty. Faust could not help but shrivel inwardly every time he visited it."

*Western Story Magazine*'s star writer was not content

at his job. Faust often complained of being "enslaved" by Street & Smith, and Frank Blackwell became literally (in his mind) a "black well" into which he dropped millions of words and many years of his life.

On the other hand, Faust was afforded a wide-open stage on which to parade the mythic products of his expansive imagination. *Western Story Magazine* gave him the opportunity to indulge his prolific talent to the full and provided a handsome annual income to support his lavish overseas lifestyle. Despite his complaints, as a one-man fiction factory, he produced some of his finest work during these fourteen years with Frank Blackwell. Work that, published in book format, continues to enthrall and entertain millions of readers to this day.

Indeed, considering his output for *Western Story Magazine* alone, Faust truly earned his title "King of the Pulps."

William F. Nolan
West Hills, California
September, 1998

# More Tales of
# the Wild West

# A LUCKY DOG

*Faust had a genuine affection for dogs. Beyond his constant passion for glorious, fast-galloping stallions, he nurtured a particular fondness for white bull terriers. He keenly appreciated their fighting tenacity and steadfast loyalty. In 1922, when the Faust family moved to Katonah, in Westchester County, New York, Faust became an enthusiastic breeder of thoroughbred bulldogs. In this off-beat story, one of two terrier tales included in the present collection—"Blondy" being the second—the protagonist, Hagger the yegg, is forced to flee from a crime in New York into the savage mountains of Colorado. A thief and would-be killer—he all but murders a sheriff—Hagger is most certainly not typical of Faust's stalwart Western heroes. He's no good on a horse, and feels miserable and out of place in the snowbound high country. Then Hagger happens upon a white bull terrier in the mountains, and their unique relationship forms the heart of this oddly touching narrative. The novelette was first printed in the October 22, 1927 issue of Street & Smith's **Western Story Magazine**. For that single weekly issue, Faust contributed fiction under three names: "A Lucky Dog" bore his John Frederick byline, part one of his serial "Pleasant Jim" was bylined as Max Brand, and part five of his "Thunder Moon—Squawman" was printed under his George Owen Baxter pen name. This marked the sixth time that **Western Story Magazine** had printed a triple-Faust combination in a single weekly issue. "A Lucky Dog" is tough and tender, sentimental but not saccharine. It is, in sum, prime Faust.*

1

# I
## "ENTRANCES AND EXITS"

WHEN AT LAST HAGGAR WAS INSIDE THE SHOP, HE paused and listened to the rush of the rain against the windows. Then he turned to the jeweler with a faint smile of possession, for the hardest part of the job was over before he had opened the door to enter the place. During the days that went before he had studied the entrances and exits, the value of the contents of the place, and, when he cut the wires that ran to the alarm, he knew that the work was finished.

So he advanced, and to conceal any touch of grimness in his approach he made his smile broader and said: "'Evening, Mister Friedman."

The young man nodded with mingled anxiety and eagerness, as though he feared loss and hoped for gain even before a bargain was broached.

"How much for this?" said Hagger, and slipped a watch onto the counter.

The other drew back, partly to bring the watch under a brighter light, and partly to put a little distance between himself and this customer, for Hagger was too perfectly adapted to his part. One does not need to be told that the bull terrier is a fighting dog, and the pale face of Hagger, square about the jaws and lighted by a cold and steady eye, was too eloquent.

All of this Hagger knew, and he made a little pleasant conversation. "You're young to be holding down a swell joint like this," he observed.

The young man snapped open the back of the watch and observed the mechanism—one eye for it and one for his customer. "About two dollars," he said. "I got this place from my father," he added in explanation.

2

"Two dollars? Have a heart!" Haggar grinned. "I'll tell you what I paid. I paid twenty-two dollars for it."

"There are lots of rascals in the business," said Friedman, and he made a wry face at the thought of them.

"I got it," said Hagger, raising his voice in increasing anger, "right down the street at Overman's. Twenty-two bucks. I'll let it go for twelve, though. That's a bargain for you, Friedman."

Mr. Friedman closed the watch, breathed upon it, and rubbed off an imaginary fleck of dust with the cuff of his linen shop coat, already blackened by similar touches. Then he pushed the watch softly across the counter with both hands and shook his head, smiling.

"You think I want to rob you. No, I want people to keep coming back here. Two dollars, maybe two-fifty. That's the limit."

"You're kidding," observed Haggar, his brow more dark than before.

"I got to know my business," declared Friedman. "I've been at it since I was ten, working and studying. I know watches!" He added, pointing: "Look at that case. Look at that yellow spot. That's the brass wearing through. It'd be hard to sell that watch across the counter, mister."

"Well, gimme the coin. All you birds. . . you all work together to soak the rest of us. It's easy money for you!"

Friedman shrugged his eloquent shoulders and turned to the cash register.

"Here you are," he said as he swung back, money in hand.

Hagger struck at that moment. Some people use the barrel of a revolver for such work; some use the brutal butt, or a slung shot of massive lead. But Hagger knew that a little sandbag of just the right weight was fully as effective and never smashed bones; fully as effective, that is, if one knew just where to tap with it. Hagger knew as well as any surgeon.

The young man fell back against the wall. His little handful of silver clattered on the floor as he went limp; for a moment he regarded Hagger with stupid eyes, and then began to sink. Hagger vaulted lightly across the counter, lowered his man, and stretched him out comfortably. He even delayed to draw up an eyelid and consider the light in the eye beneath. Then, satisfied that he had produced no more than a moment of sleep, he went to work.

He knew beforehand that there was very little value in the material displayed, compared with its bulk and weight. All that was of worth was contained in the two trays of the central case—watches and rings, and in particular a pair of bracelets of square-faced emeralds. A little pale and a little flawed were those stones, but still they were worth something.

He dumped the contents of the two trays into his coat pockets, and then he walked out the back way. The door was locked, and there was no key in it, but he was not disturbed. He braced his shoulder against it and thrust the weight home. There was only a slight scraping sound, and the door sagged open and let the rain drive in.

He was so little in a hurry that he paused to look up to the lights and the roar of an elevated train crashing past. Then he walked lightly down the street, turned over to Lexington at the next block, and caught a southbound taxi. At Third Street he stopped, and then walked back two blocks and turned in at a narrow entrance.

The tinkle of the shop bell brought a looming figure

clad in black, greasy with age.

"Hullo, Steffans."

"Hullo, Hagger. Buy or sell tonight, kid?"

"I sell, bo."

The big man laughed silently and ushered the customer into a back room. "Lemme see," he urged, and put his hands on the edge of a table covered with green felt.

"Nothing much," said Hagger, "but safety first, y'understand? Big dough for big chances. I'm going light lately."

After this apology, he dumped his loot on the table, and Steffans touched it with expert fingers.

"Chicken feed, chicken feed!" he said. "But I'm glad to have it. I could handle a truck load of this sort of stuff every day and the damned elbows would never bother me."

"Go on," said Hagger.

"You want to make a move," said Steffans. "You're always in a hurry after a job. Look at some of the other boys, though. They never attempt to leave town."

"Except for the can," said Hagger.

Steffans settled himself before the little heap and pulled his magnifying glass down from his forehead.

"That's right," he said. "You never been up the river. You got the luck."

"I got the brains," corrected Hagger. "Some saps work with their hands. Brains are what count. Brains, and crust like yours, Steffans, you robber."

"I get a high percentage," said Steffans, "but then I always mark 'em up a full value. Y'understand? I'll give you seventy on this batch, Haggar."

"Seventy for me after what I've done," sighed Hagger, "and you sit here and swallow thirty for

5

nothing!"

Steffans smiled. "I've done a couple of stretches myself," he said. "You know the dicks make life hell for me. Now, I'll give you seventy percent on this stuff. Wait till I finish valuing it."

He began to go through the items swiftly, looking aside now and then to make swift calculation, while Hagger watched in admiration. Of all the fences, Steffans was the king, for the percentage he took was high, but the prices he gave were a little better than full. So he sat in his dark little pawnshop and drew toward himself vast loot collected by second-story men, pickpockets, yeggs of all descriptions.

"This isn't so bad, kid," he said, "and I'll put the whole thing down at eleven thousand. That'll give you seven thousand and seven hundred. Take you as far as Pittsburgh, I guess?"

"It's more than I expected," said Hagger instantly. "But what do I have to take instead of cash?"

"Not a damn thing. I got a payment in just a few minutes ago. Hold on a minute."

He disappeared and came back with a bundle of paper money in his hand. Of this he counted out the specified amount and then swept all the stolen jewels into a small canvas bag.

"Is that all, Hagger?"

"That's all."

"So long, then. What was the dump?"

"No place you know, hardly likely. So long, Steffans. Here's where I blow."

He said good bye to the pawnbroker, and, stepping out onto the sidewalk, he crashed full against the hurrying form of one about to enter—a tall, young man, and by the light from within, Hagger made out the

6

features of Friedman.

It startled him. Nothing but a sort of magic intuition could have brought the jeweler to such a place in his hunt for the robber. Or had Steffans relaxed his precautions lately and allowed the rank and file to learn about his secret business?

This he thought of on the instant, and at the same time there was the glitter of a gun shoved into his face, and a hoarse voice of rage and joy sounding at his ear.

"The hand is faster than the gun," Hagger was fond of saying.

He struck Friedman to the wet pavement and doubled swiftly around the corner.

## II
## "THE TORTOISE AND THE HARE"

SOMETHING THAT STEFFANS HAD SAID NOW BROUGHT a destination to Hagger's mind, and he took a taxi to Penn Station and bought a ticket for Pittsburgh. There was a train out in thirty minutes, and Hagger waited securely in the crowd until the gatekeeper came walking up behind the bars. Gatekeeper?

"Oh, damn his fat face!" snarled Hagger. "It's Buckholz of the Central Office. May he rot in hell!" Past Buckholz he dared not go, and, therefore, he left Penn Station, regretting the useless ticket, for he was a thrifty soul, was Hagger.

There are more ways out of New York than out of a sieve. Hagger got the night boat for Albany, and slept heavily almost until the time to dock. Then he dressed in haste and went down on deck as the mass formed at the head of the gangplank.

It amused Hagger and waked him up to sidle through

7

that mob, and he managed it so dexterously that it was always some other person, rather than he, who received the black looks of those whom he jostled. He sifted through until he was among the first near the head of the broad gangplank, and the next moment he wished that he were in any other place, for on the edge of the wharf he saw the long, yellow face of Friedman, and his bright black eyes seemed to be peering up at him.

There was no use trying to turn back. At that moment the barrier was removed, and the crowd poured down, carrying Hagger swiftly on its broad current. They joined the mass that waited on the platform.

Suddenly a voice screamed: "Officer! Look! It's him!"

It was Friedman, that damned Friedman, again.

"If I ever get out of this," muttered Hagger, who habitually spoke his more important thoughts aloud, "I'll kill you!" He began to work frantically through the crowd to the side, and he saw the uplifted nightstick of a policeman, trying to drive in toward him.

Out of the mass, he began to run. He knew all about running through a scattered mob, just as he knew how to work like quicksilver through a denser one. Now he moved at such a rate that the most talented of open-field runners would have gaped in amazement to see this prodigious dodging.

He found a line of taxicabs, leaped over the hood of one, darted up the line, vaulted back over the bonnet of a second, paced at full speed down a lane, and presently sat swinging his legs from the tailboard of a massive truck that rumbled toward the center of town.

"That's all right for a breather," said Hagger, "and a guy needs an appetite, when he's packing about eight grand."

He pitched on a small restaurant and, with several newspapers, sat down to his meal. He had not touched food since the previous morning, and Hagger could eat not only for the past but for the future. He did now.

The waiter, bright with admiration, hung over the table. "What wouldn't I give for an appetite like that," he said. "I suppose that you ain't had that long?"

Hagger, looking up curiously, observed that the waiter was pointing with a soiled forefinger, and at the same time winking broadly.

What could be wrong? With the most childish asininity, Hagger had allowed his coat to fall open, and from the inside pocket the wallet was revealed, and the closely packed sheaf of bills!

He was far too wary to button it at once, and went on with his breakfast. Yet, from the corner of his omniscient eye, he was keenly aware of the tall waiter talking with the proprietor, whose gestures seemed to say: "What business is it of ours?"

What a shame that there are not more men like that in the world, to make life worth living?

He sank deeper into his papers over another cup of coffee. He preferred the metropolitan journals, for by delving into them he picked up—sometimes in scattered paragraphs, sometimes in mere allusions, but sometimes in the rich mines and masses of police news spread over many sheets—the information of the world in which he moved. So he observed, for instance, that Slim Chaffer, the second-story man, had broken jail in Topeka; and that Pie Winters was locked up for forgery in Denver; and that Babe McGee had been released because of lack of evidence. At this he fairly shook with delicious mirth. For what a guy the Babe was—slippery, grinning, good-natured, and crooked past belief! Lack of evidence?

9

Why, you never could get evidence on the Babe! Not even when he was stacking the cards on you.

To think of such a man was an inspiration to Hagger. He finished his coffee. Then he paid the bill and put down exactly ten percent for the waiter. "For you, kid," he said significantly.

Then Hagger stepped onto the pavement and walked slowly down the street, turning his thoughts slowly, meditation slackened by the vastness of his meal.

What loomed largest in his mind was:

The man was instantly identified by Friedman, from photographs, who asserted that it could be no other than Hagger, better known as "Hagger, the Yegg," whose operations in cracking safes and raiding jewelry stores are always carried out with consummate neatness and precision. The simplicity of his work is the sign of this master criminal. The police are now hard on his trail, which is expected to lead out of town.

Every word of that article pleased Hagger. Especially he retasted and relished much: "Consummate neatness," "precision," "master criminal." A wave of warmth spread through Hagger's soul, and he felt a tender fondness for the police who would describe him in such a fashion. They were pretty good fellows, along their own lines. They were all right, damn them!

He strolled on in imagination, wandering into the heaven of his highest ambition, which was to stand before the world as a great international crook, whose goings and comings would be watched for by the police of half a dozen nations. Already he had done something to expand his horizon, and a trip to England and then as far as Holland had filled his mind with the jargons of foreign tongues, but it also had filled his pockets with the weight of foreign money. So, returning one day to Europe, he would visit Italy and France, and perhaps learn a little frog-talk, and come back and knock out the eyes of the boys by slinging a little *parlez-vous*.

After all, it was going to be pretty hot, the life that Hagger led. When he thought of the fortunes that must eventually sift through his powerful hands, he raised his head a little and such a light came into his eyes that even the passers-by along the street glanced sharply at him and gave him room. For he looked half inspired and half devilish!

Something clanged down the street—a police patrol wagon—brakes screamed—men leaped to the ground. By heaven, they actually were hunting Hagger with police patrols; it seemed that he no longer was worth the pursuit of brilliant plain-clothes men. Hagger lingered a second to digest this idea and to take note of the long, eager face of Friedman.

"I'll kill that Yid!" declared Hagger, and bolted down an alley way.

Shots boomed down the lane, and the *zing* of the bullets, as they passed, made Hagger leap like a hunted rabbit. But as he darted down onto the next main street, a taxi passed, and, although it was traveling at nearly full speed, Hagger hooked onto it. For he knew every trick of traffic. At the end of two blocks, the driver pulled up and began to curse him, but Hagger departed with a laugh.

A whole block behind him were the police, and a block on a crowded city was almost as good as a mile to Hagger. He gained the railroad yards, and there slipped past three or four detectives who, he could have sworn, had been posted there to stop him. Again the heart of

11

Hagger warmed with a singular gratitude, for the police of Albany certainly were doing him proud.

"If I'd been a murderer. . . a poisoner or something, or a grand counterfeiter, maybe. . . they couldn't have done any more for me," said Hagger as he stretched himself on the rods of an express. "Nope! Not even if I'd killed the President, say, they couldn't have done any more for me."

He laughed cheerfully as the train shuddered, and then began to roll. He would have to face freezing cold at high speed, clad only in a thin suit; he would have to endure flying cinders, cutting gravel, and all the misery of that way of travel. But he knew all about this beforehand, and he knew that he could meet the pain and endure it.

So he began that journey which eventually shunted him into Denver, and he descended in ragged, greasy clothes and with a light heart to enjoy the beauties of the mountain city. But as he came out of the station yard he was aware of a vaguely familiar figure leaning against a lamppost apparently lost in thought.

It was Friedman.

### III
### "'HALT!'"

THAT FIGURE STRUCK HAGGER'S IMAGINATION AS A fist strikes across a lowered guard, for it could not be the Jew, and yet there he stood, wholly absorbed in thought, and his coat was drawn so tightly around him that Hagger distinctly saw the outline of a revolver in a hip pocket.

That removed all sense of the unearthly, and Hagger slipped away toward the center of the town, more worried than he had ever been before. At a lunch counter, he meditated on this strange adventure.

Hagger knew something about Friedman, for, when he prepared for a job, he was as thorough as could be, and his questions had brought him much information about the proprietor of the shop. There was nothing in the least unusual about his rise, for his father had owned the place before him and had educated him in the rear workroom and behind the counter. High school, a little touch of bookishness, perhaps, which generally simply unnerves a man. What was there in this background to prepare Friedman for his feat of trailing an elusive criminal more than halfway across a continent? The detectives had not stuck to the trail so long. It was Friedman alone, apparently, who carried danger so close to Hagger time and again, and the yegg touched his side, where the comforting weight of the automatic pistol was suspended. For that, after all, seemed to be the only thing to settle Friedman's hash; he rather wished that he had sent home the shot when he had spotted the young man beside the lamppost.

"I'm getting sappy," said Hagger to his coffee. "I'm getting soft like a baby, by George."

He determined to leave the railroads, for, after all, it was not so extremely odd that he had been followed, even by an amateur detective, considering that he had stuck to the main arteries of traffic. A bit of chance and good luck might have kept Friedman up with him, but, now, he would put the jeweler to the test.

Hagger left Denver that same day and walked for fifteen hours with hardly a stop. The walk beat his feet to a pulpy soreness, but Hagger ever had a soul beyond the reach of physical pain, and he persisted grimly. He spent the night in a barn, and the next morning was

13

picked up by a truck, carrying milk toward the nearest town. That brought him another twenty miles toward the nothingness of the open range, for it seemed like nothingness to Hagger's city-bred soul. His eyes were oppressed by the vastness of rough mountains, and the mountains themselves shrank small under the great arch of the sky.

To the illimitable reach of the sky itself he looked from time to time and shook his head, for the heavens which were familiar to him were little narrow strips of gray or blue running between the tops of high buildings. On an ocean trip one could escape from this lonely sense of bigness in the smoking salon or at the bar, but the loneliness was inescapable.

Vague tremors of fear, as inborn as the pangs of conscience, beset Hagger, for, if pursuit came up with him, what could he do? There was no crowd into which one could plunge, no network of lanes and alleys to receive a fugitive. He felt that he was observed from above as inescapably as by the eye of the moon, and who can get away from that, no matter how swiftly one runs?

He was lost. He was adrift in a sea of mountain and desert, only knowing indistinctly that Denver was a port behind and San Francisco a port ahead. He managed to steal rides on rickety trains that went pushing out like feeble hands into darkness, but so vast were the dimensions of this land that he felt as though he were laboring on a treadmill.

Much had to be done on foot. He bought a rifle, a stock of ammunition, a package of salt, cigarette tobacco, and a quantity of wheat-straw papers; in this manner he felt more secure in the wilderness, and although he found game scarce and rifle work very

14

different from pistol play, yet he could get enough to live on.

He had one deep comfort—that Friedman was being left hopelessly behind. He laughed when he thought of that tall, frail youth attempting to match strides with him through such a wilderness as this where a day's journey advanced one hardly a step toward the goal.

Eventually, of course, he would come out on the farther side, and a few drinks and five minutes of the glare of city lights would take from his soul the ache of the wounds that it now was receiving. So he consoled himself.

Bitter weather began to come upon him. All deciduous trees were naked, and he passed small jungles of stripped brush encased in ice. Snow fell, and once the road turned to ice when a sleet storm poured suddenly out of the black heavens. Still, Hagger kept on. He did not laugh, but he was not disheartened—he had the patience of a sailor in the days of canvas voyaging toward almost legendary shores. He had to sleep outdoors, improvising some shelter against the weather.

Once, after walking all night, he had to rest for a whole day at a village; he swallowed a vast meal and then lay with closed eyes for hours. Here he bought a horse, saddle, and bridle. But he was ill at ease in a saddle. The unlucky brute put its foot in a gopher hole near the next cross-roads town and broke its leg. Hagger shot it and carried the accouterments into town, where he sold them for what they would bring. After that, he trusted to his feet and the trains, when he could catch them. He spent as few hours as possible in towns, eating and leaving at once, or buying what he needed in a store and going on, for he knew that idle conversations mark a trail broad and black. He did not realize that his course was spectacular and strange, and that everyone would talk about a stranger who actually made a journey on foot and yet was not an Indian. He was living and acting according to his old knowledge, but he was in a new world of new men.

One day, as he was plodding up a grade toward a nest of bald-faced hills, a horseman trotted up behind him.

"Hagger, I want you!" said a voice.

Hagger turned and saw a sad-faced man with long, drooping mustache looking at him down the barrel of a rifle.

"Tuck your hands up into the air," said the stranger.

"What d'you want me for?" asked Hagger.

"Nothin' much. I'm the sheriff, Hagger. You stick up your hands. We'll talk it over on the way to town."

Hagger smiled. There was a delicious irony of fate in this encounter, and he felt that there was laughter in the wind that leaped on him at that moment, carrying a dry flurry of snow. That flurry was like a winged ghost in the eyes of the sheriff's young horse, and it danced to one side, making him reach for the reins. Still holding his rifle in one hand, he covered Hagger, but the yegg asked no better chance than this. His numbed hand shot inside his coat; the rifle bullet jerked the hat from his head, but his own shot knocked the sheriff from his horse.

Hagger stopped long enough to see scarlet on the breast of the man of the law. "If you'd known Hagger, bud," he said, "you'd have brought your friends along, when you came after me."

Behind the saddle he found a small pack of food. He took it, and, leaving the groaning sheriff behind him, he went up the trail, contented.

At the top of the next hill he paused and looked back.

16

The sheriff was feebly trying to sit up, and Hagger thought of retracing his way and putting a finishing bullet through the head of the man. However, it would waste time. Besides, the sheriff had his rifle and might fight effectively enough. So the yegg went on again, doggedly facing the wind.

The wind hung at the same point on the horizon for five days, growing stronger and colder, but Hagger accepted it without complaint. It bit him to the bone, but it acted as a compass and told him his direction. Twice he nearly froze during the night, but his marvelous vitality supported him, and he went on again and warmed himself with the labor of the trail.

It now led up and down over the roughest imaginable hills and mountains. All trees disappeared save hardy evergreens; the mountains looked black; the sun never shone; and all that was brilliant was the streaking of snow here and there.

Now and again he passed cattle, drifting aimlessly before the wind, or standing head down in the lee of a bluff, their stomachs tucked up against their backs, dying on their feet. So he did not lack for fresh meat.

Presently, however, his supplies ran out, and after that he pushed on through a nightmare of pain. He began to suffer pains in the stomach. Weakness brought blind spells of dizziness, in the midst of one of which he slipped and nearly rolled over the edge of a precipice. But it never occurred to him to pause or to turn back. Nothing could lie ahead much worse than what he had gone through.

Then, on the third day of his famine, he saw a hut, a squat, low form just visible up a narrow valley. He turned instantly toward it.

# IV
## "CLEAN FIGHTING"

SINCE THE SHERIFF HAD KNOWN OF HIM, EVERYONE IN this country might know, Hagger reflected. Therefore, he made a halt near the hut, and beat some warmth and strength into his blue hands. He looked to his automatic; the rifle slung at his back would probably be too slow for hand-to-hand work. After he had made these preparations, he marched on to the hut, ready to kill for the sake of food.

He knocked but got no answer. He knocked again, and this time he was answered by a shrill snarling. He called. The dog inside growled again.

This pleased Hagger, for he realized that the owner of the place must have left and the dog was there to guard the shack until the return of his master. When that master returned, however, he would find something gone from his larder, and something more from his wardrobe.

The door was closed, but, oddly enough, it was latched from the outside. This puzzled Hagger for a moment, until he remembered that, of course, the master of the house would have secured the door from that side in leaving. So he set the latch up, and prepared to enter.

Inside, in the meantime, the dog was giving the most furious warning, and Hagger poised his automatic for a finishing shot. He could have laughed at the thought that any dog might keep him from making free with that heaven-sent haven.

Steadying himself, he jerked the door wide and poised the pistol.

A white bull terrier came at him across the floor in a fury, but plainly the dog was incapable of doing damage. The animal staggered, dragging his hind legs. His ribs thrust through his coat, and the clenched fist of a man could have been buried in his hollow flanks. Hagger kicked him. The terrier fell and lay senseless with a thin gash showing between his eyes where the toe of the boot had landed.

Then Hagger kicked the door to and went to find food. There was very little in that hut. On a high shelf behind the stove he found two cans of beans and pork, a half moldy sack of oatmeal, and the remnant of a side of bacon. There was coffee in another tin, some sugar and salt, and a few spices. That was all.

Hagger ate the sugar first in greedy mouthfuls. Then he ripped open a can of beans and devoured it. He was about to begin on the second, when the terrier, reviving, came savagely at him, feebler than before, but red-eyed with determination to battle.

Hagger, open can in hand, looked down with a grim smile at the little warrior. He, too, was a man of battle, but surely he would not have ventured his life for the sake of a master's property as this little fellow was determined to do.

"You sap," said Hagger, "a lot of thanks he'd give you! Why, kid, I'd be a better friend to you, most likely."

He side-stepped the clumsy rush of the fighting dog and saw the terrier topple over as it tried to turn.

"You'd show, too," said Hagger, nodding wisely, because he knew the points of this breed. "You'd show and win. In New York. At the Garden. . . is what I mean."

He stooped and caught the lean neck of the dog by the scruff, so that it was helpless to use its teeth. Then he spilled some beans on the floor before it.

"Eat 'em, you dummy," said Hagger, still grinning. "Eat 'em, bare bones!"

The sight of food had a magic effect on the starved brute. Still, he did not touch it at once. His furious eyes glared suspiciously at Hagger. He was growling as he abased his head, but finally he tasted—and then the beans were gone. Gone from the second can of Hagger, too.

He went to a shed behind the house and found firewood corded there. He brought in a heaping armful and crashed it down. The stove was covered with rust, and, when the fire kindled, it steamed and gave out frightful odors. Hagger was unaware of them, for he was busy preparing the coffee, the oatmeal, and the bacon. Presently the air cleared; the fumes evaporated; and the warmth began to reach even the most distant corners of the cabin.

At length the meal was ready. Hagger piled everything on the little table and sat down to eat. He was half finished, when he was aware of the dog beside the table, sitting up with trembling legs, slavering with dreadful hunger, but with the fury gone from eyes that followed every movement of Hagger's hands, mutely hoping that some of the food would fall to its share.

It was not mere generosity that moved the man, rather, it was because his hunger was already nearly satisfied and he wished to see the terrier's joy at the sight of food. He dropped a scrap of bacon, and waited.

The dog shuddered with convulsive desire; his head ducked toward the scrap; and then he checked himself and sat back, watching the face of the stranger for permission. Hagger gaped, open-mouthed.

Faintly he sensed the cause. Having received food from his hand, the dog, therefore, looked upon him as a

20

natural master, and, being a master, he must be scrupulously obeyed. Something in the heart of Hagger swelled with delight. Never had he owned a pet of any kind, and the only reason that bull terriers had a special interest for him was that he had seen them fighting in the pit.

"Take it, you little fool," said Hagger.

Instantly the morsel was gone. The tail beat a tattoo on the floor.

"Well I'll be hanged," said Hagger, and grinned again.

When he offered the dog another bit in his hand, it was taken only after the word of permission, and the red tongue touched his fingers afterward in gratitude. Hagger snatched his hand away, looked at it in utter amazement, and then he grinned once more.

"Why, damn me," murmured Hagger. "Why, now damn me." He continued feeding the dog the bacon bit by bit. Suddenly: "You rascal, you've stole all my bacon!" cried Hagger.

The dog stood up, alert to know the man's will, tail acquiescently wagging, ears flattened in acknowledgment of the angry tone. Already there seemed more strength in the white body. Tenderness rose in the heart of Hagger at that, but he fought the unfamiliar feeling.

"Go'n the corner and lie down," he commanded harshly.

The dog obeyed at once and lay in the farthest shadow, motionless, head raised, as though waiting for some command.

But warmth and sleepiness possessed Hagger. He flung himself down upon the bunk and slept heavily until the long night wore away and the icy dawn looked across the world. Then he awakened. He was very cold from head to foot, except for one warm spot at his side. It was the dog, curled up and sleeping there.

"Look here," said Hagger, sitting up. "You're a fresh sap to come up here, ain't you? Who invited you, dumbbell?"

The terrier licked the hand that was nearest him, then crawled up and tried to kiss the face of Hagger, masked in its bristling growth of many days.

The yegg regarded the dog with fresh interest.

"Nothing but blue ribbons," he said. "Nothing but firsts. Nothing but guts," he went on in a more emotional strain. "Nothing more but clean fighting. Why, you're a dog, kid!"

The dog, sitting on the bunk, cocked its head to follow this language and seemed to grin in approval.

"So," said Hagger, "we're gonna get some breakfast, kid. You come and look!"

He went out, carrying his rifle, and the terrier staggered to a little pool nearby and licked feverishly at the ice. When Hagger broke the heavy sheet, the animal drank long. There was less of a hollow within his flanks now. Turning from the little pond, Hagger saw a jack rabbit run from a bit of brush, followed by another a little smaller.

Luck was his! He dropped hastily to one knee and fired. The rearmost rabbit dropped; the other darted toward the safety of the shrubbery, but Hagger knocked him down on the verge of the shadows.

By the time he had picked up his first prize, the terrier was dragging the second toward him, but his strength was so slight that again and again he sprawled on the slippery snow.

Hagger strode back to the hut and from there looked toward the bushes. He could see that the dog had progressed hardly at all, but never for a moment did he relax his efforts to get the prize in.

## V
## "A LOW HOUND"

THE AMUSEMENT OF THE YEGG CONTINUED UNTIL HE saw the dog reach the end of its strength and fall. Then he strode, still laughing, to the rescue, and picked up the rabbit. The terrier, panting, then managed to get to its feet and move uncertainly at the heels of its new master. Now Hagger built another roaring fire and roasted the larger of the rabbits. The second he fed to the dog while he ate his own portion. Then sleepiness came upon him the second time, for nature was striving in her own way to repair the ravages of cold and starvation in him.

When he wakened, his nerves were no longer numb, his body was light, and strength had returned to his hands. He saw that he had slept from early morning until nearly noontide. So he hastened to the door and swept the horizon with an anxious glance. He hardly cared, however, what enemies awaited him, for now that he was himself once more, he felt that he could face the world with impunity. Indeed, he looked out on no human enemy, but upon a foe which would nevertheless have to be reckoned with. The wind which had blown steadily all these days had fallen away at last, and was replaced by a gentle breeze out of the south carrying vast loads of water vapor toward the frozen north. The water fell as huge flakes of snow, some of them square as the palm of a man's hand; sometimes the air was streaked by ten million pencil lines of white wavering toward the earth; and sometimes the wind gathered strength and sent the billows uncertainly down the valley, picking the white robes from the upper slopes and flinging them on the floor of the ravine.

When he opened the door, it cut a swath in the heaped drift that had accumulated before the shack. Hagger stepped into the softness and whiteness with an oath. He saw nothing beautiful in the moth wings which were beating so softly upon the world, and he cursed deeply, steadily. "There's no luck," said Hagger. "Only the sneaks and the mollycoddles. . . they got all the luck. There ain't no luck for a man."

He was disturbed by something writhing within him, and, turning, he picked up the dog out of the drift where it was vainly struggling. The terrier was much stronger now. Still, his ribs stuck out as mournfully as ever, and his body was a mass of bumps and hollows. It would be days before strength really returned to him.

Hagger prepared himself at once for the march. His self-confidence rose proudly in spite of the labor that confronted him, and he felt his strength turn to iron and his resolution harden. In a way he loved peril and he loved great tasks, for what other living was there, compared with these crises when brain and soul had to merge in one flame or the labor could not be performed?

He had cleaned the cabin of its entire food cache, meager as it had been.

"If there was more than I could pack," declared Hagger to himself, "I'd burn it up. . . I'd chuck it out to spoil in the wet. Why, such a skunk as him, he don't deserve to have a bite left him. . . a low hound. . . that would leave a pup to starve. . . why, hell!" concluded Hagger.

This raised in Hagger an unusual sense of virtue. For by comparing himself with the unknown man who had left the white dog to the loneliness and starvation of this cabin he felt a surge of such self-appreciation as brought tears to his eyes. His breath came faster, and he reached for the terrier's head and patted it gently. The dog at once pressed closer to him and tried to rest its forepaws upon his knee, but it was far too weak and uncertain in its movements to manage such a maneuver.

It was time to depart, and Hagger walked to the door lightly and firmly.

"So long, old pal!" said Hagger to the dog, and walked away.

The snow was still falling fast, sometimes heaving in the wind and washing like billows back and forth, so that it seemed wonderfully light and hardly worth considering. But in a few strides it began to ball about his feet and caused him to lift many extra pounds with either leg. Moreover, reaching through this white fluff, he had no idea what his footing would be, and repeatedly he slipped. He knew that he had left the narrow trail, and he also knew that it would be hopeless to try to recover it. All of this within the first fifty strides since he left the door of the shack.

Then he heard a half-stifled cry behind him, like the cry of a child. It was the white dog coming after him in a wavering course—sometimes he passed out of sight in the fluff. Sometimes his back alone was visible.

Hagger, black of brow, turned and picked up the dog by the neck. He carried him to the cabin, flung him roughly inside, and latched the door.

"Your boss'll come back for you," said Haggar.

He walked away, while one great wail rose from within the cabin. Then silence.

Straight up the valley went Hagger, regardless of trail now, knowing that he must reach the higher land at the farther end quickly, otherwise the whole ravine would

25

be impassable, even to a man on snowshoes, for several days. He pointed his way to a cleft in the mountains, now and again visible through the white phantoms of the storm. The wind, rising fast, pressed against his back and helped him forward. He felt that luck was turning to him at last.

Yet, Hagger was dreadfully ill at ease; a weight was on his heart. Something wailed behind him.

"Your boss'll come back for you, you sap," said Hagger. Then he added with a shudder: "My God, it was only the wind that yelled then."

But he had lied to the dog and himself, for he knew that the man would not and could not come back, and, when he did, the terrier would be dead.

Hagger turned. The wind raged in his face, forbidding him. All his senses urged him to leave that fatal ravine. The wide, white wings of the storm flew ceaselessly against him. "You go to hell!" said Hagger with violence. "I'm gonna go back. I'm gonna. . . ." He bent his head and started back.

It was hard going through the teeth of the storm, but he managed it with his bulldog strength. He came at last to the shack once more, a white image rather than a human being, and jerked open the door. Through the twilight he had a dim view of the terrier rising from the floor like a spirit from the tomb and coming silently toward him.

Hagger slammed the door behind him and stamped some of the snow from his boots. The heat of his body had melted enough of that snow to soak him to the skin. He felt a chill cutting at his heart, and doubly cold was it in the dark, moist hollow of that cabin. He would have taken a rock cave by preference. There was about it something that made him think of a tomb—he dared not carry that thought any further.

The brave and mighty Hagger sat for a long, long time in the gloom of this silent, man-made cave. In his lap lay the head of the dog, equally silent, but the glance of the man was fixed upon eternity, and the glance of the dog found all heaven in the face of the man.

At length Hagger roused himself, for he felt that inaction was rotting the strength of his spirit. Blindly he seized the broom that stood in a corner of the shack and swept furiously until some warmth returned to his spirit and his blood was flowing again. Then he stood erect in the center of the shack and looked around him.

Already, as he knew, the snow outside was too deep to admit his escape, and still it fell, beating its moth wings upon the little cabin. He was condemned to this house for he knew not how long, and in this house he must find his means of salvation.

Well, he had plenty of good seasoned wood in the shed behind the shanty—for that he could thank heaven. He had salt to season any meat he could catch and kill. And, besides, he was fortified by two enormous meals on which he could last for some days.

The dog, too, was beginning to show effects from the nourishment. Its eyes were brighter, and its tail no longer hung down like a limp plumb line. By the tail of a dog you often read his soul.

But Hagger avoided looking at the terrier. He feared that, if he did so, a vast rage would descend upon him. For the sake of this brute he had imperiled his life, and, if he glanced at the dog, he would be reminded that it was for the sake of a dumb beast that he had made this sacrifice which, in a way, was a sacrilege. For something ordained, did it not, that the beasts should serve man rather than man the beasts?

27

If such a fury came upon him, he would surely slay the thing which had drawn him back to his fate.

## VI
## "HELP"

FOR THE SALT AND THE FUEL HAGGER COULD GIVE thanks. For the rifle, the revolver, the powder and lead he need offer no thanksgiving. He had brought them with him. With these he could maintain his existence, if only prey were led within his clutches. But first of all he must devise some means for venturing upon the snow sea.

There was not a sign of anything in the house. He remembered that some discarded odds and ends had been hanging from the rafters of the shed, and for this he started.

When he would have opened the door, a soft but strong arm opposed him, and, thrusting with all his might, he had his way, but a white tide burst in upon him and flooded all parts of the room. The wind had shifted and had heaped a vast drift against the door. He beat his way out.

Then he saw that he must proceed with patience. To that end, therefore, Hagger got from the interior of the cabin a broad scoop shovel that, no doubt, had served duty many a winter before. With it he attacked the snow masses and made them fly before him. He began to throw up a prodigious trench. The door of the shack lay at the bottom of a valley, so to speak, and now he could see that the entire roof of the house had been buried by the same drift. A gloomy suspicion came to him. He feared. . . . He hardly dared to name his fear, but hastened back into the house and kindled a fire. At once

28

the smoke rolled back and spread stiflingly through the place.

He went doggedly out, turning his head so as to avoid the sight of the dog. He climbed to the roof, that slanted so that he had difficulty in keeping a footing there, and, working busily with his shovel, he cleared the snow away.

The snowfall ceased; the bright stars came out; and their glance brought terrible cold upon the earth, much more dreadful than anything Hagger ever had endured before. He had known extremities of heat, but even the most raging sun did not possess this invisible, still-thrusting sword. Sometimes he felt as though his clothes had been plucked from his back, and as though he were a naked madman, toiling there. Numbness, too, began to overtake him, and a swimming mist, from time to time, rose over his brain and dimmed the cruel light of the stars. However, Hagger saw only one way out, and he went doggedly ahead. *Only a cur will quit. A dog shows his teeth to the end.* That was an old maxim with Hagger, who had seen the pit dogs die like that, grinning their rage, seeking gloriously for a death hold on the enemies before death unloosed their jaws.

So Hagger worked his way to the ridge of the roof. With some difficulty he cleared the chimney, and then descended to work on the fire. Bitter work was that. He laid the tinder and the wood, but, when he attempted to light a match, his cold-stiffened fingers refused to grip so small a thing. He tried to hold a match between his teeth and strike the bottom of the match box broadly across it. But he merely succeeded in breaking half a dozen. He went out into the starlight and shook the contents of the safe into the palm of his hand.

There were three matches left. No, no! Not

matches—but three possibilities of life, three gestures with which to defy the white death. Now, at last, the utter cold of fear engulfed the heart and the soul of Hagger and held him motionless in the night until something touched his leg.

He looked down and saw the raised head of the bull terrier. A new wonder gripped Hagger. After all, he was clad and the dog was thinly coated at best. He was in full strength, and the beast was a shambling skeleton. He was a man and could make his thoughts reach beyond his difficulties with hope, at least. He possessed strong hands, and so could labor toward deliverance. But the beast had none of these things, and, yet, he made not so much as a gesture of rebellion or doubt—not one whimper escaped from that iron heart of his. Silently, he looked up to this man, this master, this god. Behold, his tail wagged, and Hagger was aware of a trust so vast that it exceeded the spirit of glorious man.

Hagger stumbled back into the cabin and fell on his knees. He did not pray; he merely had tripped on the threshold, but he found the dog before him, and he gathered that icy, dying body into his arms. He felt a tongue lick at his hands. "Christ. . . Christ," whispered Hagger, and crushed the dog against his breast. Perhaps that was a prayer, certainly it was not a curse, and who knows if the highest good comes from us by forethought or by the outbursting of instinct.

But after those two words had come chokingly from the throat of Hagger, warmth came to his breast from the body of the dog, and that warmth was a spiritual thing as well. Now he stood up, and, when he tried a match, it burst instantly into flame.

Hagger looked up—and then he touched the match to the tinder—flame struggled with smoke for a moment, as thought struggles with doubt, and then the fire rose, hissed in the wood, put forth its strength with a roar, and made the chimney sing and the stove tremble while Hagger sat broodingly close, drinking the heat and chafing on his knees the trembling dog.

At length he began to drowse, his head nodded, and he slept. How late he had labored into that night was told by the quick coming of the dawn, for surely he had not slept long when the day came. The stove was still warm, and the core of the red fire lived within the ashes. The dog was still slumbering in his arms.

Hagger woke. He roused the fire and began at the point where he had left off in the starlight. That is, under a sunny sky from which no warmth but brilliant light descended, he opened the rest of his way to the shed, and there he examined the things which, as his mind dimly remembered, had been hanging from the rafter. About such matters he knew very little, but, probably from a book or a picture, he recognized the frames of three snowshoes and understood their uses— but to the frames not a vestige of the netting adhered.

When Hagger saw that he looked down to the dog at his side.

"Your skin would be what I need now," said Hagger. At this, the terrier looked up, and Hagger leaned and stroked its head, then he cast about to find what he could find. What he discovered would do very well— the half-moldy remnants of a saddle—and out of the sounder parts of the leather that covered it he cut the strips and fastened them onto the frames. It required all of a hungry day to perform this work, and, when the darkness came, his stomach was empty, indeed, and the belly of the dog clave to his back, for the terrible cold invaded the bodies of beast and man even when the fire

31

roared close by—invaded them, and demanded rich nurture for the blood.

Hagger strapped the shoes on and went off to hunt. Since the dog could not follow, he was bidden to remain behind and guard. So, close to the door he lay down, remembering, and resistant even to the glowing warmth of the stove, with its piled fuel. Hagger went out beneath the stars.

The shoes were clumsy on his feet, particularly until he learned the trick of trailing them with a short, scuffling gait. The snow had compacted somewhat, still it was very loose, and it would give way beneath him and let him down into a cold, floundering depth now and again. In spite of this, he made no mean progress, working in a broad circle around the shack, until he came to windward of a forest where the snow had not gathered to such a depth in the trough of this narrow ravine, and where the going was easy enough.

Other creatures besides himself had found this favorable ground, for, as he brushed into a low thicket on the edge of the woods, a deer bounded out. Hagger could hardly believe his good fortune and brought the rifle readily to his shoulder. Swathed in rags and plunged into his coat pocket, he had kept his right hand warm, and the fingers were nimble enough as he closed them on the trigger. Yet the deer sped like an arrow from the string, and, at the shot, it merely leaped into the air and swerved to the side out of sight behind some brush.

Hagger leaped sideways to gain another view, another shot, and, so leaping, he forgot the snowshoes. The right one landed awkwardly aslant on the head of a shrub, twisted, and a hand of fire grasped his foot. He went down with a grunt, writhed a moment, and then leaned to make examination. The agony was great, but he moved the foot deliberately until he was sure that there was no break. He had sprained his ankle, however, and sprained it severely. And that was the end of his hunting. Perhaps the end of his life, also, unless help came this way.

## VII
## "TWO MEET AGAIN"

QUICK HELP, TOO, WAS WHAT HE NEEDED, FOR THE cold closed on him with penetrating fingers the instant he was still. On the clumsy snowshoe he could not hop, and he saw at once what he must try to do. He took the shoes from his feet and put them on his hands. Then he began to walk forward, letting the whole weight of his body trail out behind.

It is not a difficult thing to describe, and even a child could do it for a little distance; whereas Hagger had the strength of a giant in his arms and hands. However, a hundred yards made him fall on his face, exhausted, and the cabin seemed no closer than at the beginning. When he had somewhat recovered, he began again. He discovered now that he could help a little by using his right knee and left leg to thrust him, fish-like, through the snow, but the first strength was gone from his arms. They were numb.

Yet he went on. When he came to the shed, it seemed to him that miles lay before him to the cabin, and, when he gained the cabin door, he looked up to the latch with despair, knowing that he never would have the strength to raise himself and reach it with his hand.

Yet, after some resting, the strength came. He opened the door, and the terrier fell on him in a frenzy of joy,

33

but Hagger lay at full length, hardly breathing. The labor across the floor to the stove was a vast expedition. Once more he had to rest before he refreshed the dying fire, and then collapsed into a state of coma.

Ⓥ Ⓥ Ⓥ Ⓥ Ⓥ

When the dawn came, Hagger had not wakened, but a loud noise at the door roused him, and, bracing himself on his hands, he sat up and beheld the entrance, with the dazzling white of the snowfield behind him, a tall figure, wrapped in a great coat and wearing a cap with fur ear-pieces. Snowshoes were on his feet, and his mittened hands leveled a steady rifle at Hagger.

"By the livin' damnation," said Hagger. "It's the jeweler!"

"All I want," said Friedman calmly enough, "is the cash that you got from Steffans. Throw it out."

Hagger looked at him as from a vast distance. The matter of the jewel robbery was so faint and far off and so ridiculously unimportant in the light of other events that suddenly he could have laughed at a man who had crossed a continent and passed through varied torments in order to reclaim seven thousand dollars. What of himself, then, who had made the vaster effort to escape capture?

"Suppose I ain't got it?" he said.

"Then I'll kill you," said Friedman, "and search you afterward. Do you think I'm bluffing, when I say that, Hagger?"

He ended on a note of curious inquiry, and Hagger nodded.

"No, I know that you'd like to bash my brains out," he said without emotion. "How did you find out about

Steffans and the amount of money. . . and everything?"

"I trailed you there, and then I made Steffans talk."

"You couldn't," said Hagger. "Steffans never talks. He'd rather die than talk."

"He talked," said the jeweler, smiling a little. "And now I've talked enough. I want to have that money and get out of here. If I stay much longer, I'll murder you, Hagger!"

Hagger knew that the man meant what he said.

"Call off that dog!" said Friedman, his voice rising suddenly.

The terrier had crawled slowly forward on his belly. Now it rose and made a feeble rush at the enemy, for it appeared that he knew all about a rifle and what the pointing of it signified.

For one instant, Hagger was tempted to let the fighting dog go in. But he knew that the first bullet, in any case, would be for himself, and the second would surely end the life of the dog. He called sharply, and the dog pulled up short and then backed away, snarling savagely.

Hagger threw his wallet on the floor, and Friedman picked it up and dropped it into his pocket.

"You ain't even going to count it?" said Hagger.

"It's all you've got," said Friedman, "and how can I ask to get back more than you have. God knows what you've spent along the road." He said it in an agony of hate and malice; he said it through his teeth, as though he were speaking of blood and spirit rather than of hard cash.

"I spent damned little," said Hagger regretfully. "I wish that I'd blown the whole wad, though."

"Good bye," said Friedman, and backed toward the door. "D'you sleep on the floor?"

35

Hagger could have laughed again, in spite of the agony from his foot—for exhaustion had made him fall asleep without removing his shoes, and now the swelling was pressing with a dreadful force against the leather. But he could have laughed to think that such enemies as he and his victim should talk in this desultory fashion, after the trail that each had covered. Those fellows who wrote the melodrama with the fine speeches, he would like to have a chance to tell a couple of them what he thought of them and their wares. This was in his mind, when he felt derisive laughter rising to his lips.

"Sure, I sleep on the floor," he said, "when I got an ankle sprained so bad that I can't move, hardly. Otherwise," he added savagely, "d'you think that you would have been able to get the drop on me so dead easy as all this? Say, Friedman, d'you think that?"

Friedman lingered at the door, taking careful stock of the thief. Hagger had no weapon at hand, therefore, he admitted carelessly: "It wouldn't have made much difference. I didn't have a bullet in the gun."

"You didn't what?"

The jeweler chuckled, and, throwing back the bolt, he exposed the empty chamber. "I lost the cartridges in the snow. I don't know much about guns," he declared.

Hagger was a little moved. After all, seven thousand dollars in cash would not give him food in the cabin or heal his injured ankle. But again he was touched with calm admiration of the shopkeeper. "Friedman," he said, "did you ever do any police work? Ever have any training?"

"No. Why?"

"Well, nothing. Only you done a pretty fair job in getting at me here."

36

"When I heard about the way you'd shot the sheriff," said Friedman, "and nearly killed him, I just started in circles from that point. There wasn't anything hard about it."

"No?"

"It just took time."

"What did you live on through the storm?"

"Hard tack. I still got enough to bring me back to town." He took a square, half-chewed chunk of it from the pocket of his great coat. "And what did you live on, Hagger?"

The sublime simplicity of this man kept Hagger from answering for a moment, and then he said: "I found a little chuck in this shack. . . ate that. . . shot a couple of rabbits."

"What'll you live on now?"

"Hope, kid," grinned Hagger.

The jeweler scanned the cabin with a swift glance, making sure of the vacant shelves and the moldy, tomb-like emptiness of the place. Then a grin of savage joy transformed him suddenly, and he began to nod, as though an infinite understanding had come to him.

"It'll take a while," he said. "You'll last a bit. And maybe your ankle will get well first."

"Maybe," said Hagger.

"And maybe the man who owns this place'll come back."

"Maybe," said Hagger.

Friedman turned his head a little, looked over the banked snows, and then at the growing clouds on the southern sky. "No," he said with decision, "I guess not."

"Not?"

"I guess not. None of those things'll happen. This looks to me to be about the end of you, Hagger."

37

"Maybe," assented Hagger.

Friedman ginned again, with a sort of terrible, hungry joy.

"You wouldn't do a murder," said Hagger curiously.

"Me? No, I'm not a fool!"

"Well. . . ," said Hagger, and left the rest of his thought unsaid.

He closed his eyes. When he opened them again, Friedman was outside the door.

"Hey, Friedman, old Friedman!" called Hagger.

The man turned and leaned through the doorway. "There's no use whining and begging," he said. "You got no call on me. You got what's coming to you, and that's all. If I were in your place, *I* wouldn't whine!"

"I want only one minute, Friedman."

"There's a storm coming. I can't wait."

"You'll rot in hell, Friedman, if you don't listen to me."

"Go on, then," said Friedman, leaning against one side of the door. "I'll listen."

"It's about the dog," said Haggar.

## VIII
## "A SPECIAL KIND OF DOG"

AT THIS THE EYES OF THE JEWELER NARROWED A little. One could see disbelief in them, but he merely grumbled: "Make it short, will you? What you driving at, Hagger?"

"This dog, here, you take a look at him. You got a liking for dogs, Friedman, I guess?"

"Me?" said Friedman. "Why should I like the beasts?"

Hagger stared. "All right, all right," he said. "You

38

don't like 'em, but this is a special kind of a dog. You know what kind, I guess?"

"A white dog," said Friedman, only interested in that he was waiting for some surprise in the speech of the yegg.

"A bull terrier," said Hagger violently. "These here . . . they're the only dogs worth while. These are the kings of the dogs. Like a gent I heard say. . . 'What will my bull terrier do? He'll do anything that any other dog'll do, and then he'll kill the other dog!'" Hagger laughed. It was a joke that he appreciated greatly.

But Friedman did not even smile. "Are you killing time?" he asked at length.

"All right," said Hagger, shrugging his shoulders. "Only what I really want to tell you is this. . . this dog'll stick by you to the limit. This dog'll die for you, Friedman!"

"He looks more like he'd tear my throat out. But, look here, Hagger, what sort of crazy talk is this? Why should I give a damn about a dog, will you tell me that?"

"You don't," said Hagger slowly as he strove to rally his thoughts and find a new turning point through which he could gain an advantage in this argument. "You don't. No, you're a damned intelligent, high type of man. You wouldn't have been able to run me down, otherwise. And you want a good practical reason, Friedman. Well, I'll give you one. You take that dog out to civilization, and you put him up for sale, what would you get?"

"Get? I dunno. Twenty-five dollars from some fool that wanted that kind of a dog."

"Yeah?" sneered Hagger. "Twenty-five dollars, you say? Twenty-five dollars!" He laughed hoarsely.

The jeweler, intrigued, knitted his brows and waited.

"Maybe fifty?"

"Five hundred!" said Hagger fiercely.

Friedman blinked. "Go on, Hagger," he said. "You're trying to put something over on me."

"Am I? Am I trying to put something over on you? You know what the best thoroughbred bull terriers fetch, when they're champions, I suppose?"

"Is this a champion?" asked Friedman.

"He is!" lied Hagger with enthusiasm.

"Champion of what?"

"Champion bull terrier of the world!" cried Hagger.

"Well," said Friedman. "I dunno. . . this sounds like a funny yarn to me."

"Funny?" cried Hagger, growing more enthusiastically committed to his prevarications. "Funny? Look here, Friedman, you don't mean to stand up there and tell me man to man that you really don't know who this dog is?"

"How should I know?" asked Friedman.

"Well, his picture has been in the papers enough," said Hagger. "He's had interviews, like a murderer or a movie star, or something like that. He's had write-ups and pictures taken of him. I'll tell you who he is. He's Lambury Rex. . . that's who he is!"

This fictitious name had a great effect upon the listener, who displayed a new interest.

"It seems to me that I've heard that name," he said. "Lambury Rex? I'm pretty sure that I have."

"Everybody in the world has," Hagger assured him dryly. "I said that he was worth five hundred. Why, any first-rate bull terrier is worth that. Five hundred! A man would be a fool to take twenty-five hundred for a dog like this. Think of him taking the first prize. . . finest

40

dog in the show. . . a blue ribbon. . . ."

"Did he do that?"

"Ain't I telling you? Say, Friedman, what have I got to gain by telling you all this?"

"I dunno," Friedman assured him, "and I see you're killing time, because what does it matter about the dog?"

"You poor fool!" shouted Hagger. "You poor sap! I'm offering you this dog to take out of the valley with you. Does that mean anything, you square head?"

Friedman said nothing for a moment and then growled: "Where do you come off in this?"

"Listen!" shrieked Hagger. "Why do I have to come off in it? Why? I offer you a dog! Talk sense, Friedman. Here's something for nothing. Here's the finest dog in the world. . . ."

Friedman cut in coldly: "And you're offering him to me?"

"I see," said Hagger slowly, nodding. "Why should I give him to you, when you've been trailing me, and all that. Well, I've got no grudge against you. I soaked you for seven thousand. You soaked me and got it back. We're all square. But the main thing is this. . . Friedman, don't you leave this dog behind to starve here in the shack with me!"

"Maybe he won't die of starvation," said Friedman. "Maybe he'll make a couple of meals for you first. Stewed dog for Hagger?" He laughed cynically, but his laughter died at once, stopped by the expression of unutterable contempt and disgust on the face of the yegg.

"Anyway," said Hagger, "that's the end of your joke. Take him, Friedman. Take him along and make a little fortune out of him. Or keep him and he'll get you

41

famous."

"Look here," said Friedman. "How could I ever get him through the snow?"

"You broke a trail to come in," said Hagger. "You could take him back the same way. He's game. He'll work hard. And. . . and you could sort of give him a hand now and then, old fellow."

Hagger was pleading with all his might. He had cast pretense aside, and his heart was in his voice.

"It beats me," repeated Friedman suddenly. He stepped back inside the shack. He sat down in one of the chairs and regarded the yegg closely—his twisted foot and his tormented face. "It beats me," repeated Friedman. "You, Hagger, you're gonna die, man. You're gonna die, and yet you're talking about a dog!"

"Why," said Hagger, controlling his temper, "will it do me any good to see a dog starve at the same time that I do?"

"Might be company for you, I should think. . . since you like the cur such a lot."

"Cur?" said Hagger with a terrible frown. "Damn you, Friedman, you don't deserve to have a chance at the saving of a fine animal like him, a king of dogs like Linkton Rex. . . ."

"A minute ago," cut in the jeweler sharply, "you called him Lambury Rex."

"Did I? A slip of the tongue. You take me, when I get excited, I never get the words right and. . . ."

"Sure you don't." The visitor grinned wide and slow. "I don't believe this dog is worth anything. You're just trying to make a fool of me. It'd make you die happier, if you could laugh at me a couple of times while you're lyin' here. Ain't that the truth?"

The yegg suddenly lay back, his head supported by

42

the wall of the shack. Now his strength had gone from him for the moment, and he could only look at Friedman with dull, lackluster eyes.

Vaguely he observed the differences between himself and the jeweler, measured the narrow shoulders, the slender hands and feet, the long, lean face, now hollowed and stricken by the privations through which the man had passed. Weak physically, he might be, but not of feeble character. He had sufficient force and determination to trail and catch up with Hagger himself—once Hagger had been detained by the dog.

"I tell you," said Hagger, "it's fate that you should have the terrier. If it hadn't been for him, you never would have caught me, Friedman."

"Wouldn't I?" said Friedman. His head was thrust out, like the head of a bird of prey. "I would have followed you around the world."

"Until you were bashed in the face!" said the yegg savagely.

"No, it was the will of God," said the jeweler, and piously he looked up.

Hagger gaped. "God?" he said. "What has God got to do with you and me?"

"He stopped you with a dog, and then he made me take you with an empty gun. It's all the work of God."

"Well," said Hagger slowly, "I dunno. I don't seem to think. Only I know this. . . if you ain't gonna take the dog away with you, then get out of here and leave me alone, will you? Because I hate the sight of your ugly mug, Friedman. I hate you, you swine!"

Friedman, on his clumsy snowshoes, backed to the door and hesitated. Twice he laid his hand upon the knob. Twice he hesitated and turned back once more. Then with sudden violence he sat down in the chair

43

again.

Hagger screamed in hysterical hatred and rage: "Are you gonna get out of here, Friedman? If I get my hands on you, you'll die before me, you and your cash! Friedman. . . what are you doin'?"

The question was asked in a changed voice, for Friedman was unlacing the lashes of his own snowshoes.

## IX
## "SPOOKY STUFF"

"WHAT D'YA MEAN? WHAT D'YA MEAN?" CRIED the yegg. "What're you takin' off your snowshoes for?"

Friedman stood up, freed from the cumbersome shoes, and eyed Hagger without kindness. "Lemme see your foot," he said, "and stop your yapping, will you?"

To the bewilderment of Hagger, Friedman actually trusted himself within gripping distance of his powerful, blunt-fingered hands which could have fastened upon him as fatally as the talons of an eagle. Regardless, apparently, of this danger, Friedman knelt at his feet and began to cut the shoe with a sharp knife, slicing the leather with the greatest care, until the shoe came away in two parts. The sock followed. Then he looked at the foot. It was misshapen, purple-streaked, and the instant the pressure of the shoe was removed, it began to swell.

Friedman regarded it with a shudder and then looked up at the set face of Hagger. "I dunno. . . I dunno. . . ," said Friedman, overwhelmed. "You talked dog to me, with this going on all the time. . . I dunno. . . ." He seemed quite shaken. "Wait a minute," he said.

Now that the shoe was off, instead of giving Hagger relief, the pain became tenfold worse, and the inflamed flesh, as it swelled, seemed to be torn with hot tongs. He lay half sick with pain.

Now Friedman poured water into a pot and made the fire rage until the water was steaming briskly. After that, he managed hot compresses for the swelling ankle, and alternately chilled the hurt with snow and then bathed it in hot water, until the pain of the remedy seemed far greater than the pain of the hurt.

Then Friedman desisted and sat back to consider his task. The moment he paused, he was aware of the howling of the wind. Going to the door, he pushed it open a crack and saw that the storm was coming over the ravine blacker than ever, with the wind piling the snow higher and higher. He slammed the door, then turned with a scowl on his companion.

"Well," said Hagger, "I know how you feel. I feel the same way. It's hell. . . and believe me, Friedman, you never would've caught me, if it hadn't been for the dog."

"If it hadn't been for the dog, I'd've been out of the valley before the storm came," declared Friedman bitterly. "It's got the evil eye, that cur!" He scowled on the white bull terrier, then he sat down as before, like an evil bird, his back humped, his thin head thrust out before him. "What do you eat?"

"Snow," said the yegg bitterly.

"Well?"

"There's deer around here. . . sloughs of 'em. I potted one last night, and it was the side jump I took to see what come of it that done me in like this." He added: "I got an idea that maybe you could get a deer for us, Friedman. For yourself and me and the dog is what I mean, y'understand?"

"I understand."

45

"Well?"

"I couldn't hit a deer."

"You can when you have to. If you couldn't hit a deer, how can you expect to hit me?"

"I know. That's bad. Well," agreed Friedman, "I'll go out and call the deer, Hagger. Maybe I could hit it, then." Armed with Hagger's automatic, Friedman went to the door. "Maybe the dog could go along?" he suggested, and snapped his fingers and clucked invitingly.

The answer of the terrier was a snarl.

"Seems to hate me," said Friedman. "Why?"

"I dunno, just a streak of meanness in him, most likely"

The touch of sarcasm in this answer made Friedman draw his thick brows together. However, the next instant he had turned again to the door.

"Head for the forest right down the ravine and bear left of that," said Hagger. "That's where I found a deer . . . maybe you'll find 'em using the same place for cover."

Friedman disappeared.

His sulkiness filled Hagger with dismay, and, shaking his fist at the dog, he exclaimed: "You're scratching the ground right from under your feet, pup. We never may see his ugly mug again!"

Meantime, he was much more comfortable. The rigorous and patient treatment given to his injured ankle had been most effective. Now blood circulated rapidly in the ankle—there was no quicker way in which it could be healed.

The dog, undismayed by the shaken hand, pricked his ears and crowded close to his master, and Hagger lay back, comforted, smiling. He let an arm fall loosely across the back of Lambury Rex and chuckled. How long would it take Friedman to come to this intimate understanding with the animal?

Indeed, Friedman might never enter that door again. Hagger himself in such a case never would come back to the cabin, housing as it did only a man and a dog. The wind still was strong, and the snow still fell. Again and again a crashing against the walls of the cabin told how the bits of flying snow crust were cutting at the wood. They would cut at a man equally well, and no one but a sentimental fool, Hagger told himself, would have done anything but turn his back to that wind and let it help him out of the valley.

In the course of the next hour he guessed that Friedman never would come back, and from that moment the roar of the storm outside and the whistling of the wind in the chimney had a different meaning. They were the dirges for his death. Calmly he began to make up his mind. As soon as the wood which now filled the stove had burned down, he would kill himself and the dog. It was the only manly thing to do, for, otherwise, there was only slow starvation before them.

Suddenly the door was pushed open, and Friedman stood in the entrance. In the faint dusk that dimly illumined the storm outside he seemed a strong spirit striding through confusion. On his back there was a sight almost as welcome as himself, a shoulder of venison of ample proportions.

"It was the deer you shot at," said Friedman, putting down his burden and grinning as the dog came to sniff at it. "I found it lying just about where you must have put your slug into it. It was almost buried in the snow."

"Did it take you all this time to walk there and back?" asked the yegg.

"No," replied Friedman slowly, "it wasn't that. When I first got out and faced the wind, it seemed to blow the ideas out of my mind. I figured that it was best just to drift with the wind right out of the ravine. And I had gone quite a long distance, when there was a howling in the wind. . . ."

"Ah?" said Hagger, stiffening a little.

"A sort of wailing, Hagger, if you know what I mean . . ."

"Yes," said Hagger. "I know what you thought, too."

"No, you couldn't guess in a million years, because I never had such a thought before. I ain't a dreamer."

"You thought," said Hagger, "that it was the wail of the dog, howling behind you. Sort of his ghost, or something, complaining."

Friedman bit his lip anxiously. "Are you a mind reader?" he asked.

"No, no," said Hagger, "but, when I started to leave the valley, I heard the same thing, and I had to come back. Maybe, Friedman," he added in a terrible whisper, "maybe, Friedman, this here dog ain't just what he seems. . . but. . . ."

"Cut out the spooky stuff, will you?" snarled Friedman. "How could a dog do anything like that?"

"I dunno," said Hagger, "but suppose that. . . well, let it go. Only he never seemed like any other dog to me, and no other dog could do to you what he's done."

"You talk like a fool!" said Friedman, his anger suddenly flaring.

"Who's the biggest fool?" sneered Hagger. "You'd have to ask the dog."

# X
## "THE TERRIER'S CHOICE"

THE ANKLE GREW STRONG AGAIN. IT SHOULD HAVE kept Hagger helpless for a month, but, by the end of a fortnight of constant attention, he could walk on it with a limp; and it was high time for him to move. The weather that had piled the little ravine with snow had altered in a single day; a chinook melted away the snow and filled the little creek with thundering waters from the mountains; the haze and the laziness of spring covered the earth and filled the air. It would be muddy going, but go they must—Friedman back to his shop in far-away Manhattan, and Hagger to wherever fate led him on his wild way.

On the last night they sat at the crazy table with a pine torch to give them light and played cards, using a pack they had found forgotten in a corner. They played with never a word. Speech had grown less and less frequent during the past fortnight. Certainly there was no background of good feeling between them, and all this time they had lived with an ever-present cause for dispute sharing the cabin with them. That cause now lay near the stove, stretched out at ease, turning his head from time to time from the face of one master to the other—watching them with a quiet happiness.

The dog was no longer the shambling, trembling thing of bones and weakness that first had snarled at the yegg. Now, sleek and glistening, he looked what Hagger had named him—a king of his kind. Two weeks of a meat diet were under his belt—all that he could eat, and days of work and sport, following through the snow on those hunts that never failed to send Friedman home with game—for the ravine had caught the wildlife like a

49

pocket, the deep, soft snows kept it helpless there, and even the uncertain hand of Friedman could not help but send a bullet to the mark—had made the dog wax keen and strong.

Now and again, briefly and aslant, the two men cast a glance at the white beauty, and every time there was a softening of his eyes and a wagging of his tail. But those looks seldom came his way. For the most part the pair eyed one another sullenly, and the silent game of cards went on until Friedman, throwing down his hand after a deal, said: "Well, Hagger, what about it?"

It was a rough, burly voice that broke from the throat of Friedman, but then the jeweler was no longer what he had been. The beard made his narrow face seem broader, and the hunts and exercise in the pure mountain air had straightened his rounded shoulders. Hagger met this appeal with a shrug of his shoulders, and answered not a word, so that Friedman, angered, exclaimed again: "I say, what about the dog. . . tomorrow?"

The keen eyes of Haggar gathered to points of light. For a moment the men stared at one another, and not a word was said. Then, as though by a common agreement, they left their chairs and turned in for the night.

The white dog slept on the floor midway, exactly, between the two.

Ⓥ Ⓥ Ⓥ Ⓥ Ⓥ

Dawn came, and two hollow-eyed men stood up and faced one another—Friedman keenly defiant and Hagger with gloomy resolution in his face.

He jerked his head toward the bull terrier. "He and me. . . we'd both be dead ones," said Hagger, "except

50

for you. You take him along, will you?"

Such joy came into the face of Friedman as nothing ever had brought there before. He made a quick gesture with both hands as though he were about to grasp the prize and flee with it. However, he straightened again. As they stood at the door of the shack, he said briefly, his face partly averted: "Let the dog pick his man. So long, Hagger!"

"Good bye, Friedman."

Each knew that never again would he be so close to the other.

They left the doorway then, Friedman turning east, for he could afford to return through the towns, but Hagger faced west, for there still was a trail to be buried by him.

And behind Friedman trotted the bull terrier. The sight of this, from the tail of his eye, made Hagger reach for his automatic. He checked his hand and shook his head, as so often of late he had shaken it, bull-like, when the pains of body or of soul tormented him.

Every day, when Friedman went out to hunt, the terrier, after that first day of all, had trailed at his heels. Habit might have accounted for choice now, but to Hagger that never occurred. In a black mist he limped forward, reaching once and again for his gun, but thinking better of it each time.

He heard a yelping behind him, and, glancing back, he saw that the terrier was circling wildly about Friedman and catching him by a trouser leg, starting to drag him back in the direction of Hagger.

Friedman would not turn. Resolutely, head bent a little, he went up the wind through the ravine as if nothing in the world lay behind him—nothing worthy of a man's interest.

Then a white flash went across the space between the two. It was the dog, and, pausing midway, he howled long and dismally, as if he saw the moon rising in the black of the sky.

There was no turning back, no pleading from Friedman, however, but, as though he knew that the dog was lost to him, suddenly he threw out his hands and began to run. Running, indeed, to put behind him the thing that he had lost.

Hagger faced forward. There was happiness in his heart, and yet, when the white flash reached him and leaped up in welcome, he was true to his contract, as Friedman had been, and said not a word to lure the terrier to him. There was no need. Behind his heels, the dog settled to a contented trot, and, when after another hour of trudging Hagger paused and sat on a rock to rest his ankle, the terrier came and put his head upon his master's knee.

All the weariness of the long trail, and all the pain of the last weeks vanished from the memory of Hagger. He was content.

## XI
## "OUT OF MISCHIEF"

HE KILLED TWO RABBITS AND A PAIR OF SQUIRRELS that day. Never had his aim been better, not even when he spent a couple of hours each day tearing the targets to bits on the small ranges in New York. He and the terrier had a good meal, and that night the dog curled up close to his master and slept.

Hagger wakened once or twice. He was cold in spite of the bed of fir branches which he had built, and the warmth of the dog's body. But he was vastly content, and, putting forth his hand, he touched the white terrier softly—and saw the tail wag even in the dog's sleep. He had the cherishing feeling of a father for a child.

When he wakened in the early dawn, he turned matters gravely in his mind. He could go back to the great cities for which he hungered, where crowds were his shelter, and whose swarms made the shadow in which he retreated from danger. But how should he get to any such retreat with the dog? How could the dog ride the rods? How could the dog leap on the blind baggage?

For some reason which he could not understand, but which was simply that the dog had chosen him, he was forced to choose the dog. It was vain for him to try to dodge the issue and tell himself that he was meant for the life of the great metropolitan centers. The fact that was first to be faced was the future of the dog. He decided, therefore, that he would take time and try to settle this matter by degrees, letting some solution come of itself.

For two days he wandered and lived on the country, and then he saw before him a long, low-built house standing in a hollow. He looked earnestly at it. There he could possibly find work. The mountain range and its winter lay whitening behind him, shutting off his trail until the real spring should come, and, in the meantime, should he not stop here and try to recruit his strength and his purse? Little could be accomplished without hard cash. So he felt, and went on toward the ranch house.

There were the usual corrals, haystacks, sheds, and great barns around the place. It looked almost like a clumsily built village, in a way. So he came up to it with a good deal of confidence. Where so many lived, one more could be employed.

He met a bent-backed man riding an old horse.

"Where's the boss?"

"G'wan to the house. He's there, of course."

He went on to the house and tapped at the door. A Negro came to the door.

"Where's the boss?"

"Wh'cha want with 'im?"

"Work."

"Well. . . I dunno. . . I'll see. What can ya do?"

"Anything."

The Negro grinned. "That's a long order," he said, and disappeared.

At length, a young man stepped from the house and looked Hagger in the eye.

"You can do anything?" asked the rancher.

"Pretty near."

"A good hand with a rope, then, of course."

"A which?" said Hagger.

"And, of course, you can cut and brand?"

"What?"

"You've never done any of those things?"

"No," said Hagger honestly, beginning to be irritated.

"Have you ever pitched hay?"

Hagger was silent.

"Have you ever chopped wood?"

Hagger was silent still.

"You'd be pretty useful on a ranch," the rancher smiled. "That's quite a dog," he added, and whistled to the bull terrier.

The latter sprang close to Hagger and showed his teeth at the stranger.

"A one-man dog," said the stranger, and he smiled as though he approved. "How old is he?" he asked at length.

"Old enough to do his share of killing."

"And you?" asked the rancher, turning with sudden and sharp scrutiny on Hagger.

Again Hagger was silent, but this time his eyes did not drop. They fixed themselves upon the face of the rancher.

The latter nodded again, slowly and thoughtfully.

"I can give work, and gladly," he said, "to any strong man who is willing to try. Are you willing to try?"

"I am," said Hagger.

"To do anything?"

"Yes."

"And your dog, here. . . I have some very valuable sheep dogs on the place. Suppose that he meets them. . . is he apt to kill one of 'em?"

Hagger stared, but he answered honestly: "I don't know."

At that there was a little silence, and then the rancher continued in a lowered voice: "I have some expert hands working on this place, and they have a great value for me. Suppose you had some trouble with them. . . would you. . . ?" He paused.

After all, there was no need that the interval should be filled in for Hagger, and he said slowly and sullenly: "I don't know!"

The dog, worried by his master's tone, came hastily before him and, jumping up, busily licked his hands.

"Get down, you fool!" said Hagger in a terrible voice.

"Hum!" said the rancher. "The dog seems fond of you."

"I got no time to stand here and chatter," said Hagger, reaching the limit of his patience. "What can I do? I don't know. I ain't weak. I can try. Rope? Cut and

55

brand? I dunno what you mean. But I can try."

The rancher looked not at the man but at the dog. "There must be something in you," he said, "and, if you're willing to try, I'll take you on. You go over to the bunkhouse and pick out some bunk that isn't taken. Then tell the cook that you're ready to eat. I suppose you are?"

"I might," said Hagger.

"And. . . what sort of a gun do you pack?"

"A straight-shooting one," said the yegg, and he brought out his automatic with a swift and easy gesture.

The rancher marked the gun, the gesture, and the man. "All right," he said. "Sometimes a little poison is a tonic. I'll take you on."

So Hagger departed toward the bunkhouse.

Ⓥ Ⓥ Ⓥ Ⓥ Ⓥ

It was much later in that same day—when Hagger had finished blistering his hands with an axe.

At that time the wife of the rancher returned from a canter across the hills and joined her husband in his library, where he sat surrounded by stacked paper, for he was making out checks to pay bills.

"Richard!" she said.

"What's happened, dear?"

"How did that dreadful man come on the place? He has a face like a nightmare!"

"Where?"

"You can see him through the window. . . and. . . good heavens!. . . Dickie and Betty are with him! Your own children. . . and with such a brute as that! I want him discharged at. . . ."

"Hush," said Richard. "Don't be silly, my dear. Look

56

at the man again."

"I've looked at him enough. He makes me dizzy with fear."

"Does a master know a servant as well as a servant knows the master?"

"What on earth are you talking about?"

"Well, my dear, when you look at the man, look at the dog."

It was a busy and tangled bit of play in which Hagger was employed in an apparent assault upon the son of the family, and, although Dickie was laughing uproariously with the fun, the white bull terrier had evidently a different view of the matter, for, taking his master by the trousers, he was attempting with all his might to pull him away from mischief.

"What a blessed puppy," said the wife.

"Aye," said the rancher, "there's more in dogs than we think."

# INVERNESS

*During the month of May, 1934, Faust mailed in a series of five new stories to his agent, Carl Brandt. They featured a lazy, devil-may-care hero called Sleeper and were aimed at the action pulp markets beyond Street & Smith's **Western Story Magazine**. In October of 1933, Faust had severed his long association with **Western Story Magazine's** Frank Blackwell—due to a lowered word rate—and was now urging Brandt to seek other outlets for his pulp fiction. With these Sleeper tales, Faust was reworking a theme he'd used in **Western Story** for his hero, Reata. Neither character packed a gun. Reata was an expert with a rope, Sleeper with a knife. Each of them rode a splendid horse. In both series, the hero seeks the help of an old peddler he calls Pop, and agrees to do the wicked fellow's bidding for a specified period as a form of "payback." The Sleeper stories were sold to a new pulp, **Mavericks**; four of them appearing in the September, October, November, and December, 1934 issues of this magazine. The fourth one, which Faust had called "Inverness," was given a gaudy new title by the editor, "Sleeper Turns Horse-Thief." I have opted to restore the original title. I chose "Inverness" because it encompasses the author's abiding love for great horses—there are two of them celebrated here—and is, at the same time, a tale that delivers its full share of fast action in the best Max Brand tradition.*

# I
## "BEHOLDEN TO A PEDDLER"

SLEEPER WAS HUNGRY. THERE WAS PLENTY OF GAME to be shot in the mountains around him, but he had neither rifle nor revolver. He had not even a fishing line or a fishhook. He might build traps to catch rabbits or the stupid mountain grouse. But that would require a day or more of work and waiting, and he was too hungry for that.

So he found a shallow stream where the sun struck through the rapid of water and turned the sands to gold. There, on a flat ledge of rock just above the edge of the stream, he stretched himself and waited. Only a thin sliver of his shadow projected into the tremor of the water, and his blue eyes grew fierce with hunger when he saw the trout nose their way upstream leisurely in spite of the swift tumbling of the little brook. They moved in their element with perfect ease, like birds in the sky. One that looked sluggish with bigness and fat disappeared in a twinkling and a flash, when Sleeper's lightning hand darted down to make the catch.

But his patience was perfect. If a bear can lie on a bank and knock salmon out of a creek, Sleeper could lie in the same manner and flick out a trout now and then. He not only supposed so but he knew it, because he had done the thing many times before in the famine days of his boyhood.

His deceptively slender body remained motionless. Nothing about him stirred except the blue glinting of his eyes. And in them was the sign of the gathered nervous tension, the piling up of electric force ready to work with the speed of a leaping spark when the moment came to make a contact.

59

Another speckled beauty drifted up the stream at lordly ease. The fish started to dissolve in a flash, but the darting hand of Sleeper flicked through the water, and from his finger tips the trout was sent hurtling high into the air, to land in the grass well up the bank.

At the lower verge of the trees which descended the mountainside and stopped a little distance above the creek, Pop Lowry halted his three pack mules and looked out on the scene below. He began to smooth his bald head and laugh, silently as a grinning wolf, when he saw this fishing going on. Yet he remained there, screened by the trees and brush, while Sleeper stood up from his rock and started to make a small fire. Expertly Sleeper cleaned the fish and broiled them over the handful of flame. He was still busy when he called out: "Why don't you show your ugly mug, Pop? I'm used to it. It won't hurt my feelings."

Pop Lowry, with a start, came suddenly out from among the trees, hauling at the lead rope of the first mule, to which the other pair were tethered. Two big panniers wobbled at the sides of this mule; heaping packs swelled above the backs of the others. Pop Lowry, shambling down the slope in his clumsy boots, waved a greeting to Sleeper, and, as he came up, he said: "How come, Sleeper? What you done with thirty thousand dollars in three days, boy? Or was it a whole week?"

A dreaming look came into Sleeper's blue eyes. Then he smiled. "If that red horse had won Saturday," he said, "I'd be worth a quarter of a million!"

"What horse?" asked Pop. His long, pockmarked face kept grinning at Sleeper, but his eyes narrowed and brightened as they strove to pierce into the nature of the youth.

"He's a Thoroughbred, Pop," said Sleeper. "And he should have won. I put my money on him over at the rodeo and watched it go up in smoke."

"You mean that you bet all that on one horse. . . on one race?" demanded Pop.

"You know how it is," said Sleeper. "It's better to stay dirty poor than be dirt rich. I mean. . . what's thirty thousand?"

"It's fifteen hundred a year income, if you place it right," declared Pop Lowry.

"If I'm going to have money, I want real money," answered Sleeper. "He was only beaten by a head, so I don't mind."

He began to eat the broiled fish, while Pop looked on in a peculiar combination of horror and delight.

Sleeper was succeeding in that task very well while the peddler filled a pipe, lighted it, then sat down on a stump to smoke.

"Supposin' that you got that two hundred and fifty thousand dollars, Sleeper, what would you do with it?" Pop asked.

"I'd get married," said Sleeper. "But I don't know who I'd marry."

"You'd get married. . . and you don't know to what girl?" shouted Lowry. "Dog-gone me, if you ain't a crazy one!"

"I don't know which one," said Sleeper. "There's Kate Williams. . . I get pretty dizzy every time I think about her. But then there's Maisry Telford. Her eyes have a way of smiling that I can't forget."

"Maisry Telford. . . why, she ain't nothin' but a little tramp. She ain't got a penny to her name," said the peddler. "You mean that Kate Williams would take you, Sleeper?"

"Perhaps she wouldn't," said Sleeper. "But there have been times when we seemed to understand each other pretty well."

"My God, she's worth a coupla millions," said the peddler. "At least, when her father dies, she is. Marry her, kid, if you got any sense at all. Maisry Telford, what's she got?"

"A good pair of hands on reins or a rifle, and a nice way with a horse or a man. She could ride all day and dance all night. She doesn't need a big house. She's at home in the whole range of the mountains. She could find you a rabbit stew in the middle of the desert, and she could find firewood above timberline in a thirty below blizzard. That's some of the things that she could do."

"Take her, then," said the peddler. "It ain't in you to have sense and marry money. It ain't in you to keep anything. What you got on you now?"

"A comb, a toothbrush, and a razor," said Sleeper. "A bridle and saddle and a horse to wear them. . . clothes to cover me. . . and a knife so that I can carve my name right up on the forehead of this little old world, Pop."

Pop began to laugh. "If I was a magician and could give you any wish, what would you ask for first?"

"A sack of bull and some wheat-straw papers," said Sleeper.

Pop Lowry, laughing still, opened one of the hampers of his first mule and produced the required articles. Sleeper accepted them with thanks, and soon was smoking.

"Why did you want me to meet you up here?" asked Sleeper. "I've been waiting a whole day."

"I was held up," said the peddler.

"What sort of crookedness held you up?" demanded

62

Sleeper. "Were you planning a bank robbery, or just to stick up a stage? Or were you bribing a jury to get one of your crooks out of jail?"

"Sleeper," said the peddler, "it's a kind of a sad thing the way you ain't got no faith in me. But the thing that I want you to do now is right up your street. It's just the breakin' of a hoss to ride."

"What kind of a horse?"

"Just a nervous sort of a high-headed fool of a stallion," said the peddler. "And four of my boys have tried their hands with him and gone bust."

"Where'd you steal the horse?" Sleeper asked.

"There you go ag'in," sighed Pop Lowry, "as though I never bought and paid for nothin' in my life. But lemme tell you where the place is. You know Mount Kimbal? Well, down on the western side there's a valley, small and snug with Kimbal Creek running through it. And back in the brush there's a cabin. . . ."

"Where the Indian lived that Tim Leary killed?" Sleeper queried.

"Right. Go there, Sleeper. You'll find the hoss there. You'll find Dan Tolan there, too, and Joe Peek and Harry Paley and Slats Lewis. Know them?"

"No."

"You'll know 'em, when you see 'em. Tell 'em I sent you."

"I just break the horse, is that all?" asked Sleeper.

"Wait a minute. The thing is to break that hoss to riding, and to deliver his reins into the hands of a gent named Oscar Willie in Jaytown. That's all you have to do, and them four will help you to do it."

"Where's the catch?" asked Sleeper.

The peddler hesitated, his small bright eyes shifting on Sleeper's face. "There's some two-legged snakes that would like to have that hoss to themselves," he said at last. "You'll have to keep your eyes open."

"How does it happen that you've never given me murder to do?" asked Sleeper, looking with disgust at the pockmarked face of the peddler. "While I'm a sworn slave to you for six weeks or so longer, how does it happen that you haven't asked me to kill somebody?"

"Why ask a cat to walk on wet ground?" said the peddler. "Why give you a murder to do and let you hang afterward? In the first place, you wouldn't do the job, no matter how you've swore to be my man for the time bein'. In the second place, there's other errands you can run to hell and back for me."

Sleeper knew that Pop Lowry was telling the truth. Pop, this mysterious peddler of the open range, was a smart man, had a head on him that turned everything into gold. Six weeks ago, when he made Sleeper his slave, he could just as well have taken money. Sleeper offered it. But Pop looked far into the future. Sleeper would have given anything to keep his friend, Bones, from hanging—only Pop Lowry could help him. And the peddler had required of Sleeper three months of his service. He would take nothing else.

So for a month and a half now Sleeper had been held by oath to do whatever Pop had ordered. So far murder had not been among his assignments. But when Pop Lowry saw a chance where murder would bring in gold, Sleeper would have to do his bidding. . . .

## II
### "UNBROKEN STALLION"

DAN TOLAN WAS BIG, NOT ABOVE SIX FEET, PERHAPS, but built all the way from the ground, up to ponderous shoulders and a bull neck, to a jaw that was capable of breaking ox-bones to get at the marrow inside them. Above the jaw, big Dan Tolan sloped away. The executive part of his body was constructed along the most generous lines, but the legislative chamber was small. He had little or no forehead, and the structure of his skull was pyramidal from behind, also, sloping upward and inward from the great bulging fleshy wrinkles at the top of his neck.

Big Dan Tolan, standing at the door of the shack with a rifle in his hands, looked with disfavor at the slender young man who stood before him. Looking past this stranger, Dan Tolan saw the horse that had carried the other to the spot, and the heart of Dan was burning with desire. Every line of that creature spoke of speed and breeding. He was sixteen hands high if he was an inch, and muscled in a way that promised even the weight of Dan Tolan a ride.

"Who are you? Whatcha want? Who sent you?" asked Tolan.

"Sleeper. To break the stallion. Lowry," said Sleeper.

Tolan blinked. Then he realized that his triple question had been answered part by part.

"Lowry?" he repeated. There was no comment from Sleeper. "So Pop Lowry sent you, eh?" said Tolan. Then, without turning his head, he called: "Hey, fellers, come out here."

They came to the door. Slats Lewis was enormously tall, vastly thin, with a pair of ears like the wings of a bat, but the other two were not remarkable in any way. They would never have been noticed in any large crowd of cowpunchers.

"This here," said Tolan, "was sent by Pop. What the hell you think of that? To break the stallion, he says!"

The face of Slats was split in two by a gaping grin. "Give him a try," said Slats. "And. . . *where* did he get that red hoss, yonder?"

"Leave that hoss alone. I seen it first," said Tolan. "You want to try your hand at the stallion, eh?" He began to grin and rub his left hip with a caressing hand.

Sleeper took note of a bandage around Slats's head, and a great purple bruise that disfigured Joe Peek's forehead. Harry Paley had all the skin off the end of his nose, and it was not the heat of the sun that had removed it.

"Sure, and why not leave him have a try at Inverness?" asked Paley.

In his eagerness, he hurried out and led the way around the side of the shack to a corral that consisted of strong saplings that had been planted in a wide circle, and strengthened with cross-pieces. It made a living corral of trees with one narrow gate.

Inside that corral was one of the finest animals that Sleeper had ever seen—a Thoroughbred bay stallion.

"Walk right in and make yourself at home," said Paley.

Sleeper climbed one of the trees and sat out on a lower branch. Inverness, having apparently turned his back to the stranger and lost all interest in him, whirled suddenly, crossed the corral with a racing stride, and bounded high into the air. His eyes were two red streaks, and his mouth gaped like that of some carnivorous beast. But he fell just short in his effort, and his teeth snapped vainly at Sleeper's leg.

There was a yell of applause from the other four.

"Come down and tackle him on his own ground," yelled Dan Tolan.

But Sleeper merely crossed his legs and rolled a

66

smoke.

"Leave him be," said Paley. "He wants to think a while, and I guess I know what's he got in his bean, all right."

"We don't need to wait for the show to start," commented Slats. "When the circus begins, the band'll start up, all right."

They went back to the shack, muttering vague comments about Pop Lowry, who had sent them a half-wit, a baby-face to do a man's work. Yet, it was very, very odd, for Pop was not the fellow to make important mistakes.

They first looked over the gold stallion that had brought the youth to them. There were plenty of features that were worth much observation. For one thing, instead of a bridle, the horse wore a light hackamore; he was guided, it appeared, without a bit at all.

"Just one of these here family pets," said Slats.

"Look out. I never seen a stallion that was no family pet," said Paley.

"I'll ride him," declared Slats.

Slats was far the best rider of them all, and they helped him put on the saddle and cinch it up. The lack of a bit troubled Slats a little, but he declared that he would have no trouble with the stallion.

In fact, the big golden beauty—which would have made almost twice the substance of racy Inverness— stood as quietly as a family pet while the saddle was being adjusted and even when Slats swung into the stirrups. After that the great stallion, Careless, did a dancing step and turn, with a whip-snap at the end of it, and Slats slid out into the air and came down in a sitting posture with a great *thump*.

Careless resumed his grazing; he showed not the

67

slightest desire to bolt. Slowly Slats got to his feet.

"Anybody *see* that kid ridin' this here?" asked Slats.

"No," said Tolan.

"Then he never *did* ride him. He brought him up here on a lead. There might be one man in the world that can ride that devil, but there ain't two."

"Hold on, Slats," said Tolan. "Ain't you gonna try ag'in?"

"Me? I've had enough tryin'," said Slats, and stalked back into the house.

The others stripped off the saddle again, and Careless kept his ears pricked as he grazed.

"There's somethin' behind all this here," declared Tolan. "Two hosses that can't be rode. And Lowry behind the both of them. What might it mean, anyway?"

"Go see how the kid's getting on with Inverness," said one.

Paley went and came back with the report that the kid had descended from his tree and now was sitting on the ground. "*Inside* the corral!" said Paley.

There was a general exclamation of wonder. "How come?" demanded Tolan.

"I dunno how come," answered Paley. "But he's sure settin' there, smokin' cigarettes, and talkin' none at all. Just whistling a little. Lullaby songs is what he's whistling. Maybe he thinks Inverness is a baby in a cradle."

They laughed a good bit at this and went back to their poker game inside the shack. As the dusk came on and they lighted a lantern, Tolan went out to the corral.

"You don't eat none till you've rode that hoss!" he shouted.

Then, coming close to the corral, he peered between the trunks of the trees and saw a sight that made the hair

68

lift on his head. A tiny spot of light caught his eye, first, and then, in the dimness beneath the trees, he was able to make out a slender form seated on the bare back of Inverness!

It was true. There sat Sleeper on the unsaddled back of Inverness, sometimes puffing a cigarette that faintly lighted his handsome face, and sometimes whistling plaintive little songs. And the stallion, moving slowly, still grazing the short grass inside the big corral, paid no heed whatever to the burden on his back.

Dan Tolan went back to the shack and stood breathless with astonishment on the threshold. "Him. . . Sleeper. . . he's on the back of that damned hoss. . . and Inverness *likes* it," he gasped.

There was a general springing up.

"Set that table for five," said Tolan, "because as far as I can see, the kid is gonna eat with the men tonight."

There was a good deal of clattering about the old stove which stood in a corner of the shack, and more jangling in setting out the tin plates and cups on the table. But through this noise, a little later, the voice of Sleeper sounded.

"All right, boys," he said. "I guess Inverness is ready to be delivered."

They poured out from the shack and found that Inverness, saddled and bridled, was dancing in the starlight before the cabin. Around him, prancing, rearing as though to strike, maneuvered the great, gleaming body of Careless.

"Go back. . . back!" called Sleeper.

Careless went rapidly back, snorting protest.

"Lie down, boy," called Sleeper.

The four staring men saw the stallion sink to the ground as though he had been a well-trained hunting

69

dog.

Then, softly, Sleeper rode Inverness back and forth, saying: "He's been broken to the bridle. He's been managed long ago. He just has to remember a few things, and then he'll be safe for a lady to ride to church."

## III
## "FOUR MEN'S FORTUNES"

WHEN SLEEPER SAT AT THE TABLE WITH THE OTHERS, Dan Tolan said to him: "How you come to handle hosses like that? Got some Injun in you, or something?"

"Hey, he's got blue eyes, ain't he?" interrupted Harry Paley. "How could he be an Injun?"

"Yeah, and I've seen blue-eyed Injun 'breeds," said Dan Tolan, scowling heavily at Sleeper. "Or maybe you got some greaser in you, kid?"

"Look for yourself," said Sleeper, smiling.

He showed his white teeth as he smiled. It was almost caressing but just a trifle feline and dangerous.

"What you mean. . . look for myself?" demanded Dan Tolan, pouring half a cup of steaming black coffee down his great gullet. He wiped his mouth on the back of his hand and left a dirty stain clinging to the stiffness of the hairs.

"Why, a fellow ought to be able to tell what other people are by giving them a look," said Sleeper.

"Yeah, and how would I know what you done to Inverness?"

"I waited till the evening came on," said Sleeper. "Horses are like men. They get lonely at the end of the day, and, when Inverness poked his head over the fence and tried to look his way out of trouble, I talked to him a

70

little."

"Now, listen to the crazy talk this kid is throwing," said Slats, and split his face exactly in half with a grin.

"He *talked* to Inverness, eh?" laughed Paley.

"I talked till I got his ears forward. Then I went inside the corral," said Sleeper. "The rest was easy. When he didn't smash me up in his first charge, I saw that he wasn't a mean horse. He'd only been misunderstood."

"He'd only been *what?*" roared Slats. "Listen to me. I was short and fat till he slammed me on the ground so hard that he made me what I am today. You mean that was because I misunderstood him?"

"Misunderstood," murmured Dan Tolan. Then he roared out: "You went and hypnotized him. . . or you give him some dope. Why don't you open up and try to tell the truth like a man? What did you do to the hoss, I'm asking."

"We had a little talk together, and then I hopped up on his back. He didn't mind at all. It just reminded him of the old days."

"What old days?" asked Dan Tolan. The other three straightened a little in their chairs.

"The old racing days," said Sleeper.

"I suppose the hoss told you that he used to be a racer?" asked Paley.

"That's right," said Sleeper. "There's a saddle mark on Inverness."

"That's a lie!" exclaimed Dan Tolan. "There ain't no mark of no kind at all on him. I been over him inch by inch."

"With your eyes, not with your hands," said Sleeper. "There's a soft saddle mark behind the withers. I felt it across the bone. A Western saddle, a regular range saddle, doesn't sit where an English saddle sits,"

71

Sleeper explained. "Inverness is a racer and a good one. He's a stake horse. . . or he ought to be."

The other four stared at one another.

"He's kidding us," said Dan Tolan, presently. "Run your hands over, Paley. Tell us something about him, will you?"

"He'd be more at home working a faro lay-out," said Sleeper.

"Hey! Hold on!" exclaimed Paley.

"Aw, he seen you somewhere at work," said Dan Tolan. "What about Joe Peek? What's the touch of Joe tell you?"

"Joe sang around barrooms and maybe at the Bird Cage Theater till his voice went back on him," said Sleeper.

"Now. . . I'll be damned," muttered Peek. "He never seen *me* on the stage, anyway."

"How'd you come to guess that?" asked Tolan, scowling in darker anger than before.

"Why, he hummed one of the songs a while ago," said Sleeper. "One of those 'love you till the seas run dry' songs. He has a husky voice. . . like a singer who took to liquor, instead of singing lessons. Besides, he keeps his clothes clean, ties his bandanna with a fancy knot, looks at his boots as though he expected to see them shine. . . and real good singers don't spoil their voices with red-eye," Sleeper wound up.

There was a silence. Peek was glaring. Then Tolan laughed. "Go on, kid," he said. "Try Slats. What's he been?"

"Murder," said Sleeper, and looked straight across the table at Slats.

The tall man stared back, his eyes pale and bright. "By God," whispered Slats, "who are you?" He pushed

72

back his chair, softly, keeping those hypnotic, pale eyes steadily on Sleeper's face.

"Leave him be," interrupted Tolan. "You done pretty well with the rest. Now what about me?"

"Before you entered the ring, or after you left it?" asked Sleeper.

Tolan started. "What. . . ?" he began. Then he paused and went on: "You could tell that by the marks on my face, maybe."

"You could've got those in barroom fights," said Paley. "No, he figgered it some other way. How, Sleeper?"

"He looks at a man's hands, instead of at his eyes," said Sleeper. "He steps short. . . he's light on his feet in spite of his weight. . . and he seems set to punch, when he stands close to a man. Besides. . . ."

"That's enough," said Paley. "Want some more, Dan?"

"Yeah," muttered Tolan. "Why not? What else do you think you know, kid?"

"It's a long yarn, I guess," said Sleeper, "and I'm tired of talking."

"*I* ain't tired," answered the big fellow. "Go and yap your damned piece and let's hear what's in it?"

"Women. . . and a good deal of dirt," said Sleeper.

"Ha!" grunted Dan Tolan, pushing back his chair in his turn.

"Wait a minute," said Slats, grinning as he laid a restraining hand on his leader's shoulder.

"Yeah, I'm O K," said Tolan. "Leave him talk. I wanna hear him yap."

"When the easy money played out, you got into some trouble that landed you in the pen," said Sleeper. "That's why you were never beaten in the ring. You got into the *juzgado* first."

There was one burst of laughter that died at once. The men were watching the white hate in the face of Tolan, and it silenced them.

"And then, afterward, you didn't give a damn," said Sleeper. "You felt that the world owed you something, and you took it with a gun. Then you got thick with Slats, and since then you've been pointing out to him that the fellow was worth shooting. . . sometimes you even help with the killings. And if. . . ."

Tolan rose to his feet, slowly.

"Wait a minute," protested Slats. "Don't go and beat him up, chief, till you find out who told him these things."

"How do you tell a skunk from a coyote? By the look of the face, mostly," said Sleeper. "Slats wears his guns so that I could hardly spot them. . . he's a professional with them. But he hasn't a brain to campaign by himself. . . he's just a knife in the hand of a boss, and his boss is Tolan, by the way Slats keeps turning to him. But Tolan knows even more about guns than he does about. . . ."

"Damn!" said Tolan, and charged.

The bulk of his headlong weight knocked Sleeper backward. Tolan's driving left hand missed Sleeper's face by sheerest chance, it seemed; but the mere wind of the blow appeared to beat him toward the floor. Over his stooping body the big man stumbled. Sleeper at the same instant was rising. His hands did something strange. Dan Tolan, lurching into the air, landed face down with a frightful crash.

Sleeper's hands dipped into Tolan's clothes; two guns flashed in his grasp as he threw them out the open door. And Tolan, rising, streaming curses and blood from a

74

cut mouth, charged with both fists smashing. In an instant he had cornered Sleeper, measured him.

"Kill him!" screamed Slats.

The blow was a powerful, straight right honestly intended to tear Sleeper's head off his shoulders. Sleeper stood there as though overcome with terror, his hands only half raised and open. Then, at the last instant, he made a frightened little gesture and whirled, as though to turn his back upon the punishment. But Tolan's arm shot harmlessly over Sleeper's shoulder, and Sleeper caught that pile-driver in a double grasp. A quick heave of Sleeper's back and shoulders converted the power of Tolan's blow into a lunge that pitched the big fellow heavily against the wall.

The shock stunned him. He dropped to his hands and knees and wavered there, dripping blood onto the floor.

The others had stopped their cheerful yelling. In a deadly silence they watched as Tolan got to his feet, staggering. With both hands he was feeling for his guns. When he found that they were gone, he breathed: "Slats, he's made a fool of me. Them hands of his jar a gent silly like a mule's hoofs. Blow hell out of him, Slats!"

But Slats did not move a hand. That was very surprising to those who knew him, most of all to Dan Tolan, until his clearing eyes saw that a bright, trembling flash of a knife lay in the flat of Sleeper's hand. It was held to the side, ready for instant use. After what he had seen, Slats would as soon have tried to dodge the stroke of a snake as the hurled point of that blade.

Sleeper was hardly breathing deeply, as he said: "Well, boys, why not all sit down and finish our coffee and cigarettes?"

They sat down in silence. Dan Tolan kept licking the

blood from his mouth. The coffee cup trembled in his hand.

## IV
## "RACE OF THOROUGHBREDS"

THE SILENCE IN WHICH THE MEN AT THE TABLE SAT was a deadly thing that moved like a sliding serpent. First they glanced at one another, and then each man looked only at his own cup of coffee or the fuming of his own cigarette, until Paley said curiously: "What's your main business, outside of taming horses and raising hell?"

He had just spoken when, outside the house, there was a faint creaking sound that made Slats jump to his feet.

"The gate to the corral!" he said.

"Inverness is leanin' against it, maybe," suggested Dan Tolan.

But the creak of the gate came again, and then a horse trotted softly, passing near the house.

Without a word, the men rushed out into the moonlight and saw a tall horse striding away with a rider flattened on his back, urging him to full speed.

A keening cry came out of all those throats: "Onslow! It's Onslow that's got him!" But no man stirred to saddle a horse and pursue. There was a good reason for that. Now that Inverness was launched beyond gunshot, like a tireless arrow, he would outstride the pursuit of any mustang.

But Careless was not a mere mustang. Sleeper cast one look at the fugitive that glimmered away into nothing through the moonlight, then snatched up saddle and hackamore and whistled as he ran out the door.

Careless came, bounding like a hunting dog when it sees the gun.

"That nag looks like he might give us a chance." Dan Tolan was inspired by the beauty of the great stallion. "Tag that gent Onslow for us, and we'll come up and smash him, Sleeper! Get your hosses, boys! On the run!"

They were already sprinting for their riding gear, as Sleeper slid the saddle over the sleek back of the stallion and pulled up the cinches. It was a light saddle, made after the range pattern but without the solid mass and weight that burdens the back of a horse and is of no use except to hold the pull of the rope when a full-grown steer hits the end of the slack. The hackamore was tossed over the head of Careless; the throatlatch was not buckled until Sleeper was in the saddle, flattening himself along the neck of the horse until he had reached the strap. Then he settled himself to the work of riding a five-mile race.

For the first few miles the fugitive, no matter how he trusted to the speed of his racer, would use that speed liberally to put a vital distance between himself and all possible pursuit. After that he was likely to slacken the pace of his stallion and save his strength against the challenge of a long distance. It was probable that he had fled away on the straight line which he intended to pursue to the end of his journey, but, as Sleeper strained his eyes before him, he knew that his task would be hopeless unless he actually caught sight of the other rider.

They were in the middle of a wide plateau around which the mountains reared, slashed here and there with many cañons. Those waterways, dry except in the flood-time of June, when the snow dissolved suddenly along the heights, offered a hundred roads opening in any direction. So Sleeper let Careless rush away with his huge, rolling stride, peering all the while at the trees that dotted the plain or the rolling ground before him.

At last, he saw a dim thing that did not approach him. The other tree-forms poured back to him with the gallop of Careless, but this object floated at a distance, coming only slowly, slowly toward him. As they drew together, he knew that the running object was a man on horseback; he had seen the silhouette as the pair reached the top of a rise with the moonlight sky beyond them to make the outline clearer.

He looked back. Behind him there was no sight of Tolan and his three men. There was no help within reach, and it would have to be a man-to-man fight, if he managed to overtake Onslow. He wished that he had had a chance to learn more about that fellow who had followed four crooks of the capacities of Tolan's gang. He wanted to hear about the man who had managed, like himself, to tame the fierce stallion and ride him away. At least, Onslow must have been a well-known enemy or his name would not have sprung instantly to the lips of the four.

One thing was certain. Such a fellow was sure to be armed to the teeth and to know how to use his weapons. And this moonlight was so bright that it would serve almost like the sun for a good gunman. Sleeper carried no firearms. Neither rifle nor revolver had been in his hands since he had been forced into the service of Pop Lowry. The commissions of that dangerous criminal were too apt to put Sleeper in the way of taking life. . . and he did not want to have the opportunity.

What seemed to lie before him was the task of riding up to a fighting man through some narrow, echoing cañon and then attempting to close with him from behind. But could Careless catch Inverness, if the fugitive preferred to flee even from a single enemy? Sleeper recalled the slender black legs of the bay horse that looked like hammered iron and the length of the rein and the vast sweep of the line from the saddle to the hocks. He shook his head. Never before had he doubted the ability of Careless to run down any horse in the world.

He looked back and saw the huge, triangular head of Mount Kimbal against the moonlit sky; he looked forward and saw the smaller heights before him chopped and slashed by ravines. Well up toward the tops of these mountains he could see the faint glow of snow under the mist that was blowing across the peaks above timberline.

Into one of these ravines the stranger entered with his horse. Sleeper followed, and after that he was under a continual strain. He had to keep his horse on the very borderline of earshot. Sight would not help him a great deal, now, because the cañon floor twisted here and there so rapidly that the towering walls of the ravine fenced through the bright sky a narrow, winding path, a sort of cow trail through the stars. To keep the other in view, Sleeper would have had to venture within fifty yards of him, a great part of the time.

They were climbing continually now. Thin noises of running water underfoot mingled with the melancholy songs of waterfalls in the distance. They were up to such a height that now there was no sign of a tree except the tough lodgepole pines which are the vanguard of the Western forest, the hardy pioneers which lay down brief generations of humus before the larger trees can find rootage. Even the lodgepole pines commenced to thin out, and just above his head Sleeper saw the bald, scalped pinnacles of the peaks, sometimes wrapped with mist, sometimes silvered over with snow and white moonlight.

Then those occasional noises ahead of Sleeper stopped. The horse knew this business almost as well as his master. It was not the first time that he had been used for the stalking of danger, and Careless put down his feet like a cat. Never a loose stone did he tread on. He trembled at sudden noises of wind and water on either side. He went with his ears pricked rigidly forward and his head turned just a trifle, as though to keep his eye on the trail and on his master at the same time. As he stole forward, his eyes blazing, his red-rimmed nostrils expanded and quivering, he seemed inspired by the eagerness of a hunting beast and an inquiring man.

The wind was against them. It blew them up the high ravine or the next accident never could have happened. As it was, there came a sudden snort in the dimness ahead of them, and the next instant Sleeper made out a horseman mounting just before him.

"Hullo!" called the voice of the stranger.

Sleeper, silently, with one pressure of his heels, made Careless leap like a panther to the kill. He saw the flash of a drawn gun. He made out the bearded features of a man. The gun boomed almost in his face, and then he sloughed himself out of the saddle and hurled himself at the other.

The impact, as he gripped the man, knocked them both headlong to the ground. Even in the air the lightning hands of Sleeper were not clenched, but he drove the edge of his palm like a blunt cleaver, again and again, against the nerve center under the pit of the

80

other man's right arm, to paralyze the man's every nerve. Then they struck the ground, and Sleeper's head banged against a rock. The world whirled madly about him. . . .

## V
## "BATTLE OF THE STALLIONS"

HE WAS AWAKE. THE WORLD NO LONGER DANCED IN crazy waves—but, as in a nightmare, he could see danger without being able to do anything about it. Not a muscle of his body would respond to his will as he watched Onslow disentangle himself and rise to his feet, staggering.

The right hand with which Onslow leaned to pick up his fallen gun could not grasp the weapon, Sleeper saw. Only his left hand still functioned, but for such a fellow as Onslow that would probably be enough. He swung about toward Sleeper, made one step toward him, and leveled the gun. This, then, was to be the last moment?

But the strangest of interruptions came. Careless, making the charge like a true war-horse, had smashed his shoulder into the beautiful bay horse and knocked him reeling. Now, recovering himself after lurching past, Careless whirled about and galloped, trumpeting with rage, straight at Inverness.

The bewilderment of Sleeper did not endure. He should have known in the first place that, if two stallions caught the scent of one another, they would be instantly fierce for battle. And, like a pair of mountain lions, the two now flung together.

The bay was fast as a flash. So was Careless. In this mutual charge they swerved past one another, rearing and striking out with their sharp forehoofs. One stroke

81

of those weapons would be sufficient to smash the heavy skull like paper.

Onslow, wildly shouting out, had whirled back toward the fighting horses. He fired, and Sleeper thought for a terrible moment that it was the bullet that knocked Careless to his knees. It was not the bullet, however, but a glancing blow from the hoof of Inverness that dropped the golden stallion. And the dark blood poured down Careless's head.

Inverness rushed in to finish his victory, but Careless still was full of brain power and battle wiles. He lurched to his feet and drove his head like a striking snake at Inverness's throat. His teeth glanced from the sleek of the other throat, only when the blood came. In a whirling tangle the two great animals swerved about.

Sleeper, more by power of prayer than through physical strength, struggled back to his feet. Onslow was rushing this way and that, trying to get in a shot that would do away with Careless without imperiling the life of Inverness. Twice he fired, but the revolver wobbled in his hand—apparently he was no two-handed gunman—and Careless went uninjured.

Drawing back a little, Careless charged Inverness, checked his attack, swerved to the side, and reared. Inverness, missing these feints, thrust in to close. But one terrible blow from a forehoof struck his side with hide-ripping force, and Sleeper distinctly heard the breaking of bones. That stroke, even though it fell upon the body, brought a human groan from the throat of the bay horse. He tried to flee, but, as he turned, a second hammer stroke clipped him across the head and laid him prone.

If Inverness were not dead, he would perish the next moment, and, then, Careless would go down under

Onslow's bullets. But at this moment Sleeper found breath to cry out. It was like calling to a wild storm, but the magic of his control over the horse was so perfect that the single cry stopped Careless and sent him wincing backward.

Onslow had turned toward the sudden voice behind him, gun in hand. A stroke from the cleaver-edge of Sleeper's palm made Onslow's left hand nerveless—the big Colt dropped to the ground. Even then, with his right arm quite useless and his left hand incapable, Onslow drove bravely in toward Sleeper. But he might as well have lunged at a will-o'-the-wisp. Sleeper dodged that attack and smashed Onslow once beneath the ear.

He did not even pause to watch the inert body drop to the ground. Onslow was still collapsing as Sleeper scooped the revolver from the place where it had fallen and sprang to see if life remained in Inverness.

The stallion was recovering, struggling to his knees feebly. Inverness stood at last with hanging head, blood dripping from his torn throat. He was badly hurt, to be sure, and made no movement to escape, even though great Careless stood on the alert, braced and ready to spring again to the battle.

Sleeper touched Inverness's torn throat. It was a mere surface wound, fortunately, and the huge swelling on the side of the horse's head was not serious. Sleeper knew that there were cracked ribs under the lump that had risen on the side of the bay. But they would heal, if the horse had rest and care.

Sleeper turned back to Onslow, as the prostrate man began to struggle on the ground, returning to consciousness. Swiftly Sleeper's knowing hands wandered over the fellow, but he found no trace of another weapon except a single pocket knife of very ordinary dimensions. When he was sure of this, he stooped and helped Onslow to his feet.

Bewildered and agape, Onslow stared about him, saw Sleeper with a wild eye, and then ran toward his horse. He seemed able to see better with his hands than with his eyes, and those hands were embracing the big stallion with a trembling love.

"There's nothing to do," said Sleeper. "Those cuts are only surface slashes. They're not bleeding much now. The broken ribs are the worst part of it. Come here, Careless."

The golden stallion came to him at once, while Onslow turned slowly. He looked from Sleeper's face to the revolver in his hand, then shook his head. "You're with Tolan?" he asked.

"No," said Sleeper. "I'm simply taking Inverness."

He scooped from the ground a bit of soft moss and laid it over the cut on his stallion's head—but the bleeding was easing. His own head rang as though hammers were at work on anvils inside it.

"And you're the thief that Tolan expected, eh?" said Sleeper. "You're the one that he knew would be on the horse's trail? You're Onslow?"

"That's my name," said the bearded man. "But I never heard of a man called a thief before because he come and took his own horse back from them that had grabbed it."

"*Your* horse?" exclaimed Sleeper.

"Sure," answered Onslow.

"I should have known," said Sleeper bitterly, "that Tolan would never be mixed up in anything but dirty work! But how do you come to own a horse like that. . . a Thoroughbred?"

"He's no Thoroughbred," said Onslow.

"He's got to be," said Sleeper, frowning as he looked over the flawless lines of the stallion.

"Mustang," answered Onslow.

"That horse!" Sleeper exclaimed. Now he heard, far away, the clangor of many hoofs in a lower ravine, a noise that blew up for a moment on a gust of wind, and was gone. "There's Tolan now," said Sleeper.

"Yeah," answered Onslow, and said no more, but waited.

"Onslow," said Sleeper. "It's a queer thing that you've told me, but somehow I believe you. If Tolan gets up here. . . ." He shrugged his shoulders.

The mist had cleared up a little, although vast piles of clouds reared on either side of the brightness, toward the moon.

"They may have heard the noise of your gun," Sleeper said. "Anyway, they're coming. Onslow, suppose we try to get Inverness out of their way, broken ribs or not?"

"D'you mean that?" demanded Onslow.

"I mean it," said Sleeper. "Take his head and walk ahead of me. There. . . through that gap and down that ravine."

It was a narrow opening in a tall wall of the cliff at the left, and through this Onslow led his stallion, looking anxiously back to see how the tall bay followed. Inverness, still with his head down, went on gingerly, stepping very short, pausing now and then as though the pain in his side were too much for him to endure.

Behind him came Sleeper and Careless—and far away the noise of hoofbeats grew constantly clearer.

# VI
## "THE STALLION'S STORY"

IN THAT NARROW VALLEY THEY HAD NOT GONE FAR when they saw, at their right, a ragged cleft in the wall of the ravine that looked hardly the thickness of a man's body, but, when Sleeper tried it, he found that both horse and man could pass into a cramped little gully that, fifty feet ahead, opened out into a sort of grass-floored amphitheater a hundred yards across, with great boulders strewn over it. The sides of this amphitheater were so steep that hardly a fly could have climbed to the top edge.

Into that retreat they passed. As the older man pointed out, they had run into a bottle. The enemy need only discover them in it, and, from the heights around, Tolan and his crew would have them entirely at their mercy. But there was nothing else to do. They sat down in the throat of the narrow entrance, after the horses had been tethered inside the gully. Onslow, his revolver resting on his knee, peered into the larger valley outside, and they waited for trouble.

Now and then they could hear, from the distance, the clattering of hoofs, fading out or approaching. Again a horse neighed, far off, a sound made mysterious by the flying echoes.

"What's this horse, Inverness, all about?" asked Sleeper.

Onslow said: "What are *you* about, partner? I don't make you out. You throw in with Tolan. . . and then you throw ag'in' him."

"I'm only a fellow who wastes his time," answered Sleeper. "Tell me about Inverness."

"Well," said Onslow, "my father was a Scotchman

86

who come over early and took up some mighty bare land that reminded him of the look of things around Inverness. . . so he called his ranch by that name. The old man made the place go, and he kept expandin' until he had a whole pile of land. It was so wild that one day a band of wild mustangs break in and run off our whole dog-gone cavvy. We chased those runaways, and we seen in the distance the leader, a big bay stallion, with black stockings on all four legs and a white star on his forehead. We run those hosses with relays until we got back our own, and then we legged it after that stallion, but we never could catch White Star. He could run from morning to night and laugh at us the whole time.

"We asked around, and tried to find out if any Thoroughbreds had been lost in that neck of the woods." Onslow shook his head. "But there wasn't none missing. It was pretty plain that piece of silk and iron was a mustang, although nobody never seen a mustang with the look of him, before. Well, he got in my blood. I couldn't sleep. He got between me and my chuck. I thinned out a lot, and all the time I was on the go, tryin' to locate him." Onslow leaned forward, one hand on his knee. He was frowning slightly as he went on with his story, plainly showing that it was the sole ambition in his life.

"If we couldn't catch him with hosses and a rope, I thought, maybe, that I could manage it by creasing him. I knew that a lot of hosses had been killed that way, because, if the rifle bullet comes close enough to the vertebrae to stun the hoss, it's likely to kill him, too. But I was a pretty good hand with a gun, and I used to practice at snuffin' the flame of a candle about as far as I could see it good. And pretty soon I felt that I could peel an apple and core it with my Thirty-Thirty. So I hit the trail, and about a month later I got a good sight of White Star. He was about half a mile away, but I wriggled and snaked along until I got close enough for a fair shot."

Onslow stopped talking for a moment. In his eyes Sleeper could see him lining the sights again for that most beautiful of all horses. Then the man went on: "My heart was so big that my ribs were busting, but, when I pulled the trigger, all the mares that were with White Star scattered, running, and the stallion dropped flat. I got up and run to him. I run as fast as I could hump it, a rope ready to tie him before he come to, but, when I reached the spot, there wasn't no need of any rope to tie him. He was dead. I'd busted his neck.

"Well, I took and stayed there, sleekin' him with my hand and looking at the brightness of his dead eyes, until he begun to turn cold. Then I went home. But I stayed sick. . . and the feel of his silk hide was never out of the tips of my fingers. There wasn't nothin' but rememberin' the finest hoss I'd ever seen. . . and he was dead."

Onslow's head drooped as he felt again the dejection of that day so long ago. His fingers spread in a gesture of emptiness.

"There was Judge Winthrop, livin' not far away, that knowed nigh everything, and I talked to him one day, and he told me about mustangs that now and then turned up like freaks in the herd. You know how a mustang mostly looks. . . always with four good legs, but roach-backed and lumpish around the head, and ewe-necked, like as not. But the judge said that all of those mustangs come over. . . their ancestors, I mean. . . with the Spaniards. And those Spanish hosses was the Arab blood or the Barb from North Africa. . . the same blood that mixed with English mares to make the English Thoroughbred. Hard livin' on the prairies and in the mountains made the mustangs a tough lot, all right. . . and it disfigured 'em a good deal. It took the shine out of them and put the devil inside in its place. But now and then one of the common mustang mares would drop a foal that was a regular throw-back to those high-headed hosses that the Spaniards brought over.

"Now, when I heard the judge talk like that, I had an idea. I'd lost White Star. I'd killed him. The only way I could bring him back to life was to make him over again. And that's what I started to do. I hunted around through the mountains till I spotted what remained of his band, and I worked until I got some of his blood that had white blazes on the forehead, although God knows none of the hosses and none of the mares looked like a patch on White Star.

"That was when I was seventeen. I'm fifty-four now. It takes about four years to bring around a generation of hoss flesh. I've been workin' at that job all the time since. There's ten generations altogether, that I kept tryin', and dog-gone me, if ever I had a sign of luck till five years ago, when I bred a skinny sawbones of a stallion to a runt of a mare, and the foal she dropped had four legs under it that looked like the legs of a deer. And he had black silk stockings on all four legs, and a white blaze, right enough, on his forehead. And when I seen him, I got my hope of what he might be.

"Well, there he is back in there. He's Inverness. I gave him that name because, at about the time he was foaled, I lost Pa's ranch. I'd spent my time breedin' hosses and dreamin' dreams, instead of working the herd. I didn't have wife nor child. . . but I had Inverness."

89

The pride showed in Onslow's face as he went rapidly on. The dejection seemed to have passed from his eyes. Even Sleeper began to be excited—for he was a true judge of horses, a lover of rare beauty in the animals. Anyone could see that Inverness was unusual.

"When he was six months old, he could outrun the herd to water," Onslow continued proudly. "When he was a yearlin', he was faster'n a streak of lightnin'. And when he was a two-year-old, I tried him under the saddle, and he went along like a dream. When I felt the wind of his gallop in my face, that was a day for me, partner! It seemed to me like fifty years of livin' meant something at last.

"Well, he was all that I had. There wasn't nothin' else. I couldn't make much money out of him here in the West, I thought, but I figgered that I could make a fortune, if only I could get him into a race on an Eastern track. So I got all the money together that I could, and I rode him East. Yes, sir, I rode him every step of the way, because I sure never could've got the price of transportation for him along the road. So I landed him at a race track near to New York. Well, when I showed him to a couple of gents that knew hoss flesh, they seemed kind of surprised. They put a jockey on his back. . . and in two seconds that jockey was ridin' air, not Inverness.

"That was where I beat myself. I'd never let a human bein' lay a strap on that colt. He loved me, but he sure hated the rest of the world. I couldn't make nothin' out of him by pettin' him and introducin' him proper to the jockeys. There was one kid that spent nigh a month gettin' familiar with Inverness. No, there was nobody to ride him, and I was a hundred and eighty pounds. . . and no hoss that ever lived could pack that much weight and

90

win a race. There was only one man could sit the saddle on him. And that happened in a funny way, because there was a stable boy that used to get pretty drunk, and, while he was plastered one day, he took and climbed up on the bare back of Inverness, and sort of lay out on him, laughin', and waitin' to be bucked off. But Inverness, he never turned a hair! Later on, that feller put a saddle on him. . . and still Inverness took to him real kind.

"The boy begun to train him and give him regular gallops, and him and Inverness got real thick. One day there was a regular stake horse havin' a trial spin around the track, early in the morning, when Cliff. . . the stable boy. . . was ridin' Inverness, and they just hooked up and had it out with one another, and after two furlongs Inverness was about five lengths ahead, and the other jockey pulled up and said that his hoss was lame. But he wasn't lame. . . he was just sick, Inverness had gone away from him so fast.

"After that, Cliff, he came and told me about himself. When he was a kid, he'd been a fine jockey, but he hadn't gone straight, and he'd been ruled off the track for life for the pullin' of a hoss. He was pretty heavy now, weighin' close to a hundred and fifty. But he says it was twelve years before that he'd been ruled off, and, if he changed his name and got thinned down, he'd sure never be recognized. So I agreed with him, and he went to work. I never seen a fellow starve himself so faithful. If Cliff ever gave trouble to the world, he sure made up for it by the trouble he made for himself then. Yes, sir. He stripped the flesh off his body by ten pounds at a time and got himself down to less than a hundred and twenty.

"It was the fag end of the season when we moved off

to a Florida track, and Cliff registered himself under his new name. We put Inverness in a little no-account race, and the money I'd made, workin' in the stables, we took and bet on Inverness at ten to one. Well, sir, it was just over a mile, that race, and after half a mile was gone, Cliff had to pull his arms out to keep Inverness back. Inverness, he run the last three furlongs with his chin right on his chest and won by half a dozen lengths."

The fire was in Onslow's eyes as he visualized again that first real race. He was well warmed to his subject now, and he could hardly tell his story rapidly enough. Sleeper listened patiently—not breaking in at all, as if any sign or sound from him would somehow spoil the story or cause Inverness to lose out eventually.

"It made some talk, that race, and, when we entered Inverness in the Lexington Stakes, some of the papers begun to write about him," Onslow continued. "There was folks said that maybe he was one of the finest hosses that had ever been kept under cover, and why had a four-year-old like that never been run before, and maybe he was not able to stand trainin'. Him with legs of steel! But they all said that no matter how good he was, he would never be able to beat the great champion, Black Velvet, or his runner-up, Galleon.

"So we put down our money. And when the Lexington Stakes was run, it was a mile and a half, and the eight hosses that went out for it, they had pedigrees longer'n your arm, but not a dog-gone one of them had pedigrees that went back to Cortés, I reckon. Anyway, Galleon done the leading till they was in the home stretch, and then the champion, Black Velvet, he come with a great run, and everybody yelled for him and the crowd it went crazy, because nobody noticed that outsider, Inverness, what came right up with Black

Velvet into the lead.

"A furlong from the finish, I seen Cliff let Inverness go. He come in three lengths ahead of Black Velvet, and there wasn't no sound heard, except the hoofs of the hosses and some groanin' noises.

"Well, sir, we collected our money and felt pretty rich, but then Cliff. . . he couldn't hold himself no longer. He got drunk and started talkin'. Pretty soon he was called up by the president of the club, and they said that Cliff had been ruled off the track before and he sure was ruled off double now. . . and I was ruled off because I'd let Cliff ride. . . and Inverness was ruled off because he'd let himself be ridden.

"But there come a gent by the name of Mister Oscar Willis, and he asked me what was I gonna do with Inverness. I said that I would take him out West and start breedin' ag'in, and try to establish the line of Inverness as clear as a trout stream. And he said that he had a place in Kentucky, and he would be mighty pleased to own Inverness. He offered five thousand, and ten thousand, and fifteen to get Inverness for his breedin' farm, but I wouldn't let him go.

"So I come on West with my hoss, and I headed across country with Inverness to go back and see could I buy a chunk of the old ranch to start the breedin' farm ag'in. The first night out, I stopped at a deserted shack, leavin' Inverness hobbled outside. And when I woke up the next mornin', Inverness, he was sure gone! I never laid eyes on him ag'in until tonight."

When he had finished his long story, Onslow packed a pipe and lighted it.

"They must've stolen the horse to send it along to this fellow Oscar Willis in Jagtown," said Sleeper. "If he offered you fifteen thousand, he must have offered

Tolan and the men behind Tolan as much as twenty-five thousand. Tolan would do ten murders for half that much coin. You and I are nowhere near out of the woods now, Onslow."

"Anyway," said Onslow, "the dawn's comin' up now, and we're gonna have a chance to see a few steps of our way a mite clearer, before long."

The short summer night was, in fact, already ending. When Sleeper looked up, he could see a faint glow in the sky, with the tops of the cliffs ink-black against it. Then Onslow touched his arm.

"They're comin', partner! Look. . . look at the whole four of them."

Sleeper, turning his head with a start, saw four riders moving slowly up the floor of the outer ravine in single file.

## VII
## "BOTTLED WITH DEATH"

ALL THE HORSES DROOPED WITH WEARINESS—THE riders, however, rode erect and alert. It was plain that Dan Tolan had well-picked men with him. At the head of the procession, Dan seemed about to lead the line of riders straight on past the entrance to the amphitheater, but, when he was almost by it, he turned suddenly in the saddle and looked fixedly toward the crevice in the wall of the ravine, where Onslow and Sleeper lay stretched out flat, barely venturing to peer out at this approaching danger. Then Tolan turned his horse and rode straight for the entrance to the gap!

He was within fifty feet of the crevice before he halted as suddenly as he had started, and surveyed the entrance to the chasm from head to foot, as though making sure that it could not extend to any depth into the rock. After that, with a twitch of the reins, he pulled around the head of his horse and went up the ravine.

As the other three riders followed him as before, Onslow turned to Sleeper with relief. "That's finished," he said.

"Maybe not," said Sleeper. "We ought to get out of here. Tolan traced us this far, and he's not apt to give up now."

"How will he find us?" asked Onslow. "He sure missed us just now. He ain't a bird with wings, to hop over the mountains and look into this here bowl of ours. Partner, we found the right place. . . and I'm gonna stay here till I've got Inverness healed and right again."

After all, there was more of an instinctive than a reasonable objection working in Sleeper's blood. Therefore, he was willing to be persuaded.

The sun had come up, actually thickening the shadows that sloped from the eastern side of the hollow, although all the heights began to blaze with light and above them the piled clouds were burning. Then the sun was darkened. Thunder boomed from the central sky, and a tremendous downpour began. The duskiness of twilight took the place of the morning brightness. Hail rattled like a continual musketry, and then the rain settled in for five tumultuous minutes. It beat up clouds of water mist from the rocks. It closed the eyes with its volleys.

The thunder shower ended as quickly as it had begun. The sun once more parted the clouds. The hollow began to flash with a great brilliance, for the sunlight was reflected across the wet walls of the amphitheater.

Onslow and Sleeper, drenched by the water that had been bucketed over them, went into the hollow to find the horses. Careless, undepressed by the torrents, whinnied softly to his master, but poor Inverness seemed broken in spirit. His wounds were telling on him.

They got wisps of grass, twisted them hard, and used these to brush Inverness dry. He winced when the pressure came anywhere near the swollen place on his ribs. It had grown larger, this swelling, and it was hot to the touch.

They were still discussing the stallion, when a gun spoke from the crevice that led into the hollow. The sound seemed to fly around and around Sleeper's brain. He heard the whizzing of no bullet and yet the shock was as great as though the lead had been driven straight into his flesh. Another rifle rang out on the height above them, and Sleeper looked up in time to see the marksman drop down behind a rock. He made out Paley's checkered shirt.

Onslow said: "They've got us, partner! They've uncorked the bottle, and they've cracked it. We're gonna leak out and go to waste!"

It was obviously true. Sleeper, looking wildly about him, saw that the clouds were heaping higher and higher, rolled by the wind. It seemed to him that they represented the danger which was about to overwhelm him. He had been in many perils before this time. But never had he been so completely helpless. The mouth of the crevice was stopped against their retreat. On the heights above them was at least one rifleman, who needed only to take his time, moving around and around the edge of the upper bowl in complete security until he had a chance to pick off the two men, one by one, who might scuttle for a time to the refuge of one boulder and then another.

Dan Tolan's bawling voice boomed through the valley: "Sleeper! Hey! Sleeper!" he was calling.

"Ready, Dan!" Sleeper sang out.

At this, there was a chorus of laughter from three throats. They had manned the crevice in full force and detailed only one marksman to take the heights and command the situation from the inside.

"Well, kid," said Dan Tolan, "looks like you been playin' both ends ag'in' the middle. You wanted to get Inverness for yourself, eh?"

"I seem to be here with him," said Sleeper.

"He's gonna be here without you or Onslow, before long," bawled Dan Tolan.

"Tolan," said Sleeper, "you want two horses. They'll be dead before you get the men that are with them." He added, loudly: "Onslow, put a bullet through the head of Careless to show them that we mean what we say."

He had not needed to wink at Onslow as he spoke. The latter had not stirred to draw his Colt.

But Tolan's yell broke in: "Wait a minute. Maybe we can make some kind of terms with you *hombres*."

"What sort of terms?" asked Sleeper.

"Talk it out. Talk it out," pleaded Onslow softly. "There's gonna be another cloud burst in a minute, and then maybe we can do something."

"We could manage to maybe let one of you gents go free," called Tolan, "if we got the two hosses."

"Which one would you let go free?" asked Sleeper.

"We'd let you loose, kid," said Tolan instantly.

"Because poor Onslow might trail his horse and locate it as stolen goods?" asked Sleeper.

"Hold on," growled Onslow. "I ain't gonna be a spike in your coffin, Sleeper. . . if that's what they call you. Take your chance when it comes to you. Maybe it ain't

97

gonna come twice!"

Sleeper, turning suddenly, looked straight into the older man's blue eyes. "Two men can always die better than one," he said. But he added, more loudly: "How could I trust you, Tolan?"

"Come up here to the gulch," answered Tolan. "One of us will come out and meet you. You can have his gun for a kind of passport through us. And once you're away. . . to hell with you! We'll have something to tell Pop Lowry about his number one boy!"

"Talk it out," urged Onslow. "There's a lot of rain hangin' up there, ready to let go all holts!"

A vast thunderhead was leaning over the hollow at the moment, increasing the height of its towers, darkening its great masses.

"Tolan, it's a hard thing for me to walk out on a poor fellow like Onslow. What have you got against him?" asked Sleeper.

"He's tied up to more money than he knows about," said Tolan. "The buzzards have gotta eat him now, Sleeper. You oughta be able to see that for yourself, if you got any real sense."

One of the other men said something that Sleeper could not catch. Then Tolan called out: "We ain't gonna wait here and chatter all day. Say yes or no, Sleeper."

Sleeper looked despairingly up at the clouds that were piling in the middle sky. Then a wild impulse made him sing out: "To hell with you! I'll take my chances with Onslow."

"Are you clean crazy?" howled Tolan.

A booming of thunder broke in between them, and then Sleeper heard Slats Lewis say distinctly: "Sure, all of them extra smart guys has got a screw loose somewhere."

That instant a hornet song sounded near Sleeper's head, and a lead slug splattered against the face of the boulder before him. He looked vaguely at the white spot that had appeared on the weathered rock. But, at that moment, the rain fell with a great crash that resounded through the valley like the sound of giant hands struck together.

## VIII
## "ANOTHER DEBT PAID"

THROUGH THE NOISE OF THAT DOWNPOUR, HEAVY AS IT was, the clang of the rifle sounded once. Then the rifleman on the height was as helpless as though he were shooting down into deep water. Even Onslow had become a dim, sketchy figure before Sleeper's eyes.

But Onslow was calling: "Now, Sleeper! Let's rush 'em! Give 'em the charge, old son! Right straight for the mouth of the crevice!"

He was untethering Inverness as he spoke, and the poor, wet, beaten stallion crowded close to him like a huge child. Careless, also, was loosed in a moment. He, too, would keep at the heels of his master.

It was obvious that this was a chance, however slender. Sleeper reached out and gripped Onslow's wet hand. Then he turned and ran lightly for the entrance to the gap.

It was like running through a dream. He could not see the walls of the amphitheater or the ground three steps before him, and he almost struck the sheer wall at the end of the hollow, instead of the passageway for which he had aimed. In two quick sidesteps he flung into the open where he stood staring through the storm. He saw nothing but the dull shimmering of the descending

99

torrents of the rain. Then a yellow streak flashed twice before his eyes. There was no humming of bullets, only the booming of the reports. He dived at the figure that he made out, half risen from behind a rock.

"They're here!" yelled Joe Peek.

Sleeper's weight struck him. With his arm curved over his head like the ridge of a helmet, with a hard, sharp elbow Sleeper struck his man full in the soft pit of his stomach and seemed to feel the bone of his arm jar against Peek's spinal column. The fellow went down without a sound, folding up like a jackknife over Sleeper, cushioning his headlong fall.

As he disentangled himself, Sleeper heard a gun barking from behind him. He had a glimpse of a dim figure that ran in, firing at every step. It was the gallant Onslow, coming to the attack.

Before the old fellow reached him, Onslow suddenly staggered to the side and went down. Other guns had been answering him. Through the wet came the pungent, stinging smell of the gunpowder, and the drifting smoke made the gloom even darker. In the tight space Sleeper could just make out big Dan Tolan and the tall, meager Slats Lewis.

Only one thing was possible, and that was to strike immediately. But to rush into the blaze of those two deadly guns was like jumping into the open mouth of death. Sleeper, leaping for a jutting point of rock above his head, felt the head of a grazing bullet sear his ribs. An inch closer to his heart would have taken his life. But he swung from the rock like an acrobat from a bar—and hurled his lithe body right at the heads of the two outlaws.

Both guns blasted at his face as he shot through the air—and both bullets missed the mark. His flight from the rock had been too great a surprise for Tolan and Lewis. Straight and true Sleeper's flinging body hit the mark. He tried to strike Slats's throat with his cleaver-edged palm, hard as a pine plank, but the fighter's long jaw, solid as stone, turned back the crashing blow and numbed Sleeper's hand.

Sleeper managed to catch Slats about the shoulders and drag him down on the ground. His hands were busy as he fell. In a combat of death, the hand must be as swift as the brain that manages it, and Sleeper's brain was a little quicker than the wink of lightning. So, even in falling, he struck twice, hard, against the side of Slats's neck. Those were finishing strokes. Slats lay inert on the rocks, and Sleeper whirled to grapple with Tolan.

He was too late by the fraction of a second. Tolan, heaving himself half erect after he had been knocked sprawling, hurled himself at Sleeper and caught him with one vast, mighty arm that pinioned both of Sleeper's arms to his side. Beaten down on his face, pinned by the great bulk of Tolan, Sleeper turned his head and had a glimpse of the convulsed murder grin above him. He saw Tolan's hand raised with a rock clutched in the fingers. He saw the bucketing rain running on the big man's face. Then he received, not the brain-shattering crash of that falling stone, but a soft, inert, lifeless weight. And the report of a gun boomed heavily in his ears.

Hands grasped and raised him.

"How is it, Sleeper? Did I hurt you?" shouted Onslow.

Sleeper, staggering, but erect, laughed happily. "He's finished, Onslow. You've turned the trick!"

"Me?" said Onslow. "I was only a second chance.

You're the wildcat that counted for 'em."

Blood was running down Onslow's face from a scalp wound, but he was not seriously hurt by the bullet that had floored him. He turned the heavy body of Dan Tolan on its back, but Tolan was dead. A .45 caliber slug had drilled straight through his body. Slats Lewis lay still as a stone. Peek was beginning to groan feebly, as Sleeper and Onslow hurried out to the ravine beyond. With the horses behind them, they started down the ravine.

Ⓥ Ⓥ Ⓥ Ⓥ Ⓥ

Mr. Oscar Willis, seated on the verandah of the hotel in Jagtown, leaped suddenly to his feet and ran down to the street. A great, golden stallion was walking toward the hotel, ridden by a man who led a more slenderly made bay with the fine lines of a hawk in the air.

The stranger said, as he saw Willis: "You're Oscar Willis?"

"That's my name, and that horse. . . ?" began Willis.

"My job is to give you the reins of Inverness," said Sleeper, "and here they are."

Willis grasped the leather with a strong hand. He was a big, fat, rosy-faced man, and now laughter began to bubble in his throat. "The money. . . ," he started to say, when a bearded fellow stepped up to him and said: "Hello, Mister Willis. You don't need to hold my hoss for me. Unless maybe you think that you're receivin' stolen goods?"

Willis, staring at Onslow's face, dropped the reins with a groan, and then, from some unannounced impulse, hoisted his fat hands in the air as though a gun had been held under his nose. The fellow on the golden

102

stallion grinned very broadly. "It's all right, Willis," he said. "The murders you caused won't be pinned on you. But you better take a train for points East. This part of the world won't like you very long."

Ⓥ Ⓥ Ⓥ Ⓥ Ⓥ

Sleeper was far away from the riotous village of Jagtown when he saw, again, the tall, shambling peddler, Pop Lowry, coming down a trail. They met at an elbow turn, and Pop Lowry turned gray with rage.

"I thought you was to work for me for three months!" he exclaimed. "And here you been and give away the hoss I sent you for."

"What's the matter?" asked Sleeper. "I got the horse you sent me for, and I put his reins into Mister Willis's hands. That's what you asked me to do."

Pop Lowry, stifled, helpless with rage, glowered for an instant at his lieutenant. Then he strode on down the trail, wordless, dragging his lead mule behind him. Long after he was out of sight the light, mocking music of the bridle bells came chiming back to Sleeper's ears.

103

# CRAZY RHYTHM

*"Crazy Rhythm" appeared in the March 1, 1935 issue of Frank A. Munsey's **Argosy**. A Munsey publication, **All-Story Weekly**, had been Faust's initial home in the pulps back in 1917, and he became a regular contributor to **Argosy**. Only Street & Smith's **Western Story Magazine** ran more Faust tales—and, starting in 1935, when he was no longer producing fiction for Street & Smith, the bulk of his pulp fiction appeared again in **Argosy**, including the first Dr. Kildare serial in 1938. Since it was written in 1933, "Crazy Rhythm" might have been rejected by Frank Blackwell at Street & Smith. It was the occasional practice of Faust's agent to send on Western material rejected by Blackwell to **Argosy**, and this could have been the case here. Why would **Western Story Magazine** have turned down "Crazy Rhythm"? Not enough action, perhaps. Its ex-con protagonist, having killed in the past, is going home to find honest work, not further gun play. Thus, the story is basically a character study. Faust was feeling restricted and hemmed in by having to conform to the rules set down by Blackwell. In 1933, he was anxious to break away; the lower word rate gave him an excellent reason for doing so. "Crazy Rhythm" represents Faust's exploration of new ground within the Western genre.*

## I
### "BACK FROM PRISON"

WHEN JIMMY GEARY CAME IN SIGHT OF YELLOW Creek again, he sat down on a pine log beside the road and stared at his home town, from the old mill at one end to the house of the Bentons on the hill, with its thin wooden spires pointing up above the trees. Best of all, he could mark the roof of Graham's Tavern beyond the rest of the houses. It was still painted red, but the wave of climbing vines had thrown a spray of green across the shingles since he had last sat in the cool of the bar room and smelled the pungencies of whiskey and the pleasant sour of beer.

Behind him, following taller than the mountains, around him thicker than the trees, before him more obscuring than the morning mist, he felt his eight years of prison. Eight years out of twenty-six is a long time. Prison monotony had made everything about those years dim except their length; the distinct moments of his life, so clear that he felt he could mark them in every day of his past, continued to that moment when he had seen the card come out of Tony Spargo's sleeve. Of course, he knew that there were card cheats, but it had seemed impossible that big, beautiful Tony Spargo, so rich in eye and color and song, could actually be doing dirt for the sake of a fifteen-dollar pot. Gus Warren, at the same table, too, magnificent of brow and manner, or the Mexican with the wide face of a Chinese idol, might have been suspected, but never Tony.

He had shouted in a voice that tore his throat and cast a redness over his eyes, then he had grabbed the Colt that Tony had flashed and pulled his own gun. The weight of two bullets jarred Tony Spargo in his chair like two blows of a fist. But they were all in cahoots, the three of them. Oñate came in with a knife; Gus Warren's gun had stuck and came out only with a sound of tearing cloth. He turned his shoulder to the knife thrust and got Warren right in the middle of the face.

105

Afterward, he had to shift the gun to his left hand to settle with Oñate. But Oñate and Spargo didn't count very much; he got fifteen years for Gus Warren, and murder in the third degree. But the warden was a fine fellow, and for good behavior there is time off.

Thinking of the past cleared the mist from his mind so that he began to see what was around him and found that his hand was stroking the smooth of the log on which he sat. There were a lot of those barkless logs waiting to be dragged away, and they were still yellow-white with the blaze of axe strokes glittering like metal here and there. He looked about at the standing trees— the lower trunks mossed over on the north side and spiked with the stubs of broken branches, then came ragged, down-hanging boughs, and finally the fresh green of the top. On the opposite slope all he could see was the ranged and compacted mass of the treetops.

Men were like that, for the daily crowds of them seemed strong and happy, and it was only when one got underneath the first impression that the mold of the time and the scars and the breakings of the years could be seen.

Something disturbed Jimmy Geary. He found that it was the noise of wind in the trees and water in the creek, both exactly the same and both trying to hurry him away, as it seemed, into some unknown expectancy of action. He looked along the scattering line of logs that so many hand strokes of labor had laid there, and down the hills he stared again into the valley. There was plenty of open country with little rusty spots of color scattered over the green. Those were the cattle.

"You've got a good, clean pair of eyes in your head," the warden had told him, "but the only way for a man to keep clean is to work. In the old days you worked with a gun. You'd better find different tools now." Well, he knew the feel of the tools he wanted to manage—the rough of a forty-foot rope and the braided handle of a quirt and the oily sleekness of bridle reins. He knew cows pretty well, and now he would work with them. Finally, he would have a herd of his own, and on the fat of this land the cattle would multiply.

"I'm going to punch cows," he had told the warden, who had answered: "That's good. Anything's good, but don't try it at home. You'd better not go back there. Home towns are bad for bad boys, Jimmy. You know what I mean by that. It's bad to get a wheel into an old rut."

The warden was a wise man, and he meant that it was best for a man with a past to try a new deal at a new table. Now the eyes of Jimmy Geary were taking hold on the picture of Yellow Creek so confidently that he felt a sort of kind recognition shining back to him from the whole valley.

He got up and walked on with the loose and easy action of a very strong man whose weight has not yet become a burden. He could feel his strength pull up the calf of his leg and bulge along his thighs, and he kept partially gripping his hands to set his arm muscles in action. His eyes shone with the glory of his fitness. Fifteen years of hard labor had been his sentence, but eight years of daily companionship with a sledge-hammer had been enough. He had been pretty soft in the old days, and now he felt that softness of the body was like poison in the belly or fool ideas in the head—a thing to be purged away. As he swung down into Yellow Creek, he realized that from his sixteenth to his eighteenth year he had never dared to enter any town without at least the weight of one gun under his coat.

107

Now his hands would have to do.

He went happily down the main street's windings. The roar of the creek was off to the left, the music for which he had wakened and harkened vainly through the dark of so many nights. Slater's barn was there near the road, the brown-red of the paint peeling off it in larger patches than ever. The building was a grim outline to him because he had had that half-hour fight with Jeff Wiley behind the barn till Mexican Charlie was frightened by the great splattering of blood and ran yelling to bring grown-ups to end the battle. From that great, crimson moment, Jeff and he had felt that they were set off from the rest of the boys in Yellow Creek with a greater destiny in promise for them. It was a sign and perhaps a prophecy, when Jeff was thrown by a bucking horse and broke his neck on a Monday; for on Friday there had occurred the triple killing in Graham's Tavern that sent Jimmy up the river for eight years.

Beyond the barn, the houses were closer together. He knew them all by their own faces and the faces, the voices, the characters of the people who passed through the front doors. Another twist of the way brought him in view of the central section of Yellow Creek, the irregular "square," the flagpole in the middle of it, the boardwalk that ran around the square in front of the buildings. Everything in Yellow Creek was here, from the newspaper office to the Hay, Grain, and Coal sign of Thomas Masters, the old crook. Not very many people were moving about. There never were many people in Yellow Creek, except for holidays, and it was hardly strange that no one noticed young Jimmy Geary when he returned at last, not until after the sheriff had greeted him.

It was the same sheriff, on the same roan horse. The

sheriff had been quite an old man of forty, those eight years ago, but by a strange chance he seemed younger than before to Jimmy Geary. He pulled up his mustang so hard that the water jounced and squeaked in the belly of the broncho. He waved a silent greeting; Jimmy's salute was just as still.

"Staying or passing through?" asked the sheriff, and all the calm virtue of Jimmy vanished at a stroke.

"Whichever I damn' please!" he replied. The sheriff said nothing. He simply took in Jimmy with a long look, then jogged on down the street.

Right after that a shrill sound approached Jimmy Geary. It was almost like the barking of a dog, but it came from the lips of a thirteen-year-old boy who was capering and yelling: "Hey, everybody! Hey, turn out and look sharp! Jimmy Geary's back! Jimmy Geary's back!"

Other boys heard the cry. They came in swirls of dust. As they gathered in numbers they got closer to Jimmy. They began to laugh because crowds of boys have to do something, and that laughter was acid under the skin of Jimmy. The youngest of children can make the oldest of sages wince, if it keeps on laughing long enough.

Someone burst through the crowd. He was in such a hurry to get to Jimmy that he kept on sidling and prancing after he reached him. This fellow represented the *Morning Bugle*, he said. But he could not have represented it long, because he had been in the West only long enough for its sun to redden the end of his nose. He looked incomplete and wrinkled and uncomfortable like a man on a picnic. He wanted, he said, a few good bits from Jimmy Geary.

"I'm not talking," said Jimmy. He had learned at the

penitentiary to say that.

"You're not talking?" cried the reporter. "But you've *got* to talk! Outside of the waterfalls and the lumber mill, you're the only thing in Yellow Creek that's worth writing up. If you don't talk for yourself, other people are going to talk for you."

"How do you know me?" asked Jimmy.

"Hey, look at the spread we gave you five days ago," said the reporter. He was so proud of that spread that he carried it around with him, and now unfolded the front sheet of the *Bugle*. It was not a very big paper, but the headline could be read easily right across the square.

# JIMMY GEARY FREED

Underneath it ran the long article. Jimmy's eye picked out bits of it and put the bits away in his memory. He was the hero of the famous triple killing at Graham's Tavern. He was dangerous; he was a youthful and a smiling killer. But above all, the question was, what would his career be when he got free from the prison to his home town? Or did he intend to return to it?

"What're you gonna do?" asked the reporter. "What's the career ahead of you?"

"Cattle," said Jimmy. Then he turned his eyes from the sun-burned nose of the other and went off down the street. He had a vast desire to take the yipping boys, two at a time, and knock their heads together. He had been almost overcome by an intense need to punch out the red nose of the reporter.

People were hard to take, and that was perfectly certain. In a prison one's fellow humans are not so free to be annoying.

110

When he came to the Hay, Grain, and Coal sign of Thomas Masters, he got away from the growing crowd by stepping into the office. Old Masters sat in his usual corner with the same white whiskers bulging out of the same red face. It looked like a picture surrounded with the smoke of an explosion. He put out a fat hand, tentatively, for Jimmy Geary to grasp.

"Well, James," said Masters, "what can I do for you today?"

"Tell me where to find a job," said Jimmy.

"There are only a few good jobs, and there are a lot of good men," said Masters.

"Sure there are," admitted Jimmy. "I don't care what I get so long as there are horses and cows in it."

"And guns?" asked Masters.

"I'm traveling light," smiled Jimmy.

"You try the Yellow Creek air on yourself for a week, and then come in to see me," answered Masters, and raised his pen over a stack of bills.

Jimmy went out without a good bye because a good bye was not wanted. When he reached the sidewalk, Reuben Samuels got hold of him out of the increasing mob of boys and took him into the Best Chance saloon. He said: "I'm going to do something for you, Jimmy."—and sat him down at a small table in the back room. Samuels ordered two whiskies. Jimmy changed his to beer and then looked across the foam past the red length of Samuels's nose into the brightness of his little eyes.

"I've got a good break to offer you, and you're going to have it," said Samuels. "I've got a place up the line that used to make big business for me. Faro, roulette, or anything the boys want. But I had some trouble up there. Some of the roughs thought the faro layout was

111

queer one night, and they started smashing things up. What I need is a headliner to draw the crowd, and a bouncer well enough known to throw a chill into the boys that go around packing hardware. Well, you're the man for both places, so I could pay you double. I mean something big, Jimmy. I mean fifty or sixty a week."

Jimmy Geary shook his head. "Not interested," he said.

"Or seventy," said Samuels.

"I'm not carrying any hardware myself," said Jimmy.

"Make it eighty, then, for your health."

"Not for me."

"Ninety dollars a week for an easy job, a sitting job, most of the time. . . and, when the work comes, it's the sort of thing that's play for you. Don't say no. I'm not pinching pennies. I'll call it a hundred flat!"

Jimmy looked hard into the little eyes. "Aw, to hell with you!" he said, and arose.

"Wait a minute," said Samuels hastily. "How did I know what you are taking in your coffee? Don't run away in a huff. I'm going to do you good, I said, and I meant it. Sit here for five minutes. My cousin Abe is right here in town. One of the smartest men you ever met, Jimmy. He wants to see you."

Abe was like Reuben in the face, but his clothes were fitted to the sleek of his body more carefully. They seemed to be painted on him. His collar was so tight that his neck overflowed it and rubbed a dark spot of sweat or grease onto the knot of his tie. At the same time that his fat fingers took possession of Jimmy's hand, his eyes took brotherly possession of Jimmy's heart and soul.

"It's something big," he said to Jimmy. "I got the idea, when I heard that you were turned loose. I burned up the wires to New York. You see, I know Lew Gilbeck of Gilbeck and Slinger. They've put over some of the hottest shots that ever burned a hole in Broadway. They're reaching around for a big musical comedy spectacle to put out this fall, and I shoot them this idea over the wires. Jimmy Geary, hero of a three-man killing eight years ago, just out of prison. Big, handsome, loaded with it. Did his shooting eight years ago, when the phonograph record was playing 'Crazy Rhythm.' Give him a number where he does the thing over again. 'Crazy Rhythm' for a title. Booze. A girl or two. A real Western gunfight in the real Western way done by one who's done it before. I shoot this idea to Lew Gilbeck and he wires back. . . 'Yes, yes, yes. . . get him.' I wire back. . . 'How much? This baby won't be cheap.' He hands me back. . . 'Offer one fifty a week.' And there you are, Jimmy, with one foot already on Broadway and the other ready to step. . . ."

Jimmy Geary went with lengthening strides out of the cool shadows of the Best Chance saloon. In the dazzling brightness of the outer sun, he fairly ran into the stalwart form of Lowell Gerry, the rancher.

"Mister Gerry," he said, blocking the way, "you've always got a place for a man out on your ranch. Let me go out there and try to earn my keep until I'm worth real pay, will you?"

The sun-lined and squinting face of Lowell Gerry did not alter a great deal; one expression had been cut into that brown steel long before and it could not change. "Step aside a minute, will you, Jimmy?" he asked quietly.

Jimmy stepped aside, and Gerry walked straight past him down the street with an unhurrying stride.

Time was needed before the fullness of that affront

113

could be digested. Jimmy was still swallowing bitterness, when he got across Yellow Creek to Graham's Tavern. Even the trees around the tavern threw shadows ten degrees cooler than those which fell in any other part of Yellow Creek. Ivy grew around the watering troughs; ampelopsis bushed up around the wooden columns of the verandah, swept over the roof of it, almost obscured the windows of the second story, and so poured up in thinner streaks across the red shingles above. It was all just as pleasant as before, but there was more of it. Therefore, it was rather a shock when he found in the saloon an unfamiliar face behind the bar, instead of the fat, pale, amiable hulk of Charlie Graham. This fellow was the red-copper that a man picks up on the open range. He looked as if he had exchanged chaps for a bar apron hardly the day before. In the old days the hearty voice of Charlie was always booming, making the echoes laugh, but the new man had reduced his conversation with three or four patrons to a mere rumble.

"Where's Charlie?" asked Jimmy.

"He's in hell with Tony Spargo," said the lean bartender, and his eyes fixed as straight as a leveled gun on Geary's face.

"They don't have the same hell for men and rats," answered Geary. "Give me a beer, will you?"

The bartender paused as though about to take offense. Slowly he drew the beer and carved off the rising foam as he placed the glass on the perforated brass drain. Slowly he picked up Geary's money and made the change.

"Have one yourself," said Jimmy.

"Yeah?" queried the other, in doubt. But he saved the change and took a small beer.

"The Grahams are out of this, are they?" asked Jimmy.

"The girl's got it. Kate runs it," answered the bartender. He gave a somber nod of recognition and swallowed half of his drink. Jimmy rushed his down with a certain distaste. He wished it had been whiskey, because coming into this room had brought about him all the past and all its appetites.

"Where's Kate now?" he asked, thinking back to her. At eighteen, a lad cherishes his dignity. He had only a dim memory of red hair and spindling body, for Kate had been only about sixteen and, therefore, hardly worthy of a glance.

She was out back, said the bartender, so Jimmy went through to the rear. He stopped in the small card room. It was just the same. The little phonograph stood on the corner table where it had played "Crazy Rhythm" eight years before. The same pair of colored calendars decorated the walls. On a chair rose the pile of newspapers from which men helped themselves when they were tired of cards or growing a little world-conscious. Then he crossed to the table at which he had sat. It was even covered with the same green felt. He could remember the V-shaped cut on one edge of the cloth. Behind the chair where Tony Spargo had sat, there was a half-inch hole bore into the wall. Until he saw it, he had forgotten that the first bullet had drilled right through Tony's powerful body. It was strange that life could be knocked out by a flash of fire and a finger's end of lead.

Then he went out behind the house and saw a red-headed girl of twenty-three or four, peeling potatoes. She had three pans for the unpeeled, the peelings, and the peeled. She wore rubber gloves through which the

115

flesh appeared duskily. She should have been very pretty, but there was no smile about her. What a man sees first is the light behind a picture; after that he sees the picture itself. Well, you had to look closely at this girl before you saw that she was pretty.

"You're Kate Graham?" he asked.

"Hello, Jimmy," said the girl. "Welcome home. I've got your old room fixed up. Want it?" She slid the pan of peelings onto a chair and stood up. She had plenty of jaw and plenty of shoulders, but her strength remained inside the sense of her femininity as in a frame. She had a smile, too, but it was no glare for heavy traffic—there were dimmers on it. It invited you close and promised to keep shining, for a long time. A door opened in Jimmy, and something like a sound moved through him.

"Yes, I want the room," he said, looking at her. "Tell me how about Charlie, if you don't mind?"

"A whiskey bat and pneumonia did the rest," she answered.

"Whiskey's hard on the eyes, all right," said Jimmy. "I was mighty fond of Charlie."

"Were you?" asked the girl.

"Yeah, I sure was."

He kept hesitating until it suddenly occurred to him that he had no words for what he wanted to say. He hardly knew what he wanted, either, except he wished to see that faint brightening about the eyes and mouth. He said he could find the way to the old room, so he left her and went off up the stairs that creaked in all the familiar places. It was wonderful that he should remember everything so well. From sixteen to eighteen he had written himself "man" and kept a room here and lived—well, without too much labor.

When he got up to the room, he heard snoring inside

116

it. He backed off and looked at the number to make sure. It was Number Seventeen, all right, so he opened the door softly and looked in. A long man with a jag of beard on the chin and a sweep of mustaches across his mouth was lying on the bed with his mouth open. It was Doc Alton.

That sight brought up the past on galloping hoofs. He crossed the room. Doc opened his eyes and shut his mouth.

"Hello, Jimmy," he said quietly. Doc was always quiet. Perhaps that was why he had been able to open so many safes without bringing on the vengeance of the law. He had been one of those aging men of forty, eighty years ago. Now he looked to the altered eye of Jimmy Geary even younger than in the other days, as the sheriff had. Doc sat up and shook hands.

"How's everything?" he asked.

"All right," said Jimmy. "Thanks for the letters and the cash."

"They wouldn't let me send much," answered Doc. "Feeling like work?"

"Listen to me!" said Jimmy fiercely. "Wake up and listen! When I brace people around here for an honest job, they give me the eye and walk straight past. But the thugs come and hunt me up. . . Samuels, and that sort, and a safe-cracker comes and waits in my room. I say . . . what the hell?"

Doc Alton yawned. "You feel that way about it? All right. I'll take a snooze here. I'm kind of tired. If you ain't changed your mind before you're ready to go to bed, I won't argue with you any, but I've got a sweet layout fixed up. It's a two-man job, and it's fat. There ought to be fifteen, twenty thousand in it."

"No, and be damned to you!" said Jimmy. "I'm going

117

out to get an honest man's job."

"Take a gun along with you, then," said Doc Alton. "Let me tell you something. A lot of people around here remember Tony Spargo."

"A dirty louse of a cardsharper!" answered Jimmy Geary. "To hell with him, too, and the crooks that remember him." He strode from the room and had sight, from the door, of Doc Alton yawning again, his eyes already closing for more sleep. At the stable he hired a saddle horse and hit out over the rough trails to the ranches. He put in the rest of that day getting to eight ranch houses, and he collected eight refusals.

Two of them stood out. Old Will Chalmers said to him: "What sort of a plant are you aiming to fix on me out here? No, I don't want you or any three like you, either." At the Morgan place, the girl he had known as Ruth Willet opened the kitchen door for him. He had gone to school with Ruth, and he put out his hand in a pleased surprise. She simply slammed the door in his face, and screeched from behind it: "I've got men in this house, Jimmy Geary. You get out of here, or I'm gonna call 'em! I got men and guns here. You get off this place!"

That was his last try. He got off the place and went slowly back to Graham's Tavern, letting the cowpony dog-trot or walk, letting the evening gather off the hills and slide unheeded about him. Darkness, also, was rising out of his heart across his eyes.

He put up the horse in the barn and went into the saloon. There was no one in it except the bartender, although voices were stirring in the back room.

"Whiskey!" he said, looking down at his watery reflection in the bar varnish.

"How's things?" asked the bartender cheerfully.

118

Jimmy Geary lifted his eyes with deliberation across the shining white of the bar-apron and over the lean face of the other. There he rested his glance for a moment, drank the whiskey, and lowered the glass to the bar again without changing his gaze. "You take a run and a jump and a guess at how things are," said Jimmy Geary.

"Yeah?" said the bartender. But he worked a smile back onto his face. "Look here," he murmured, "there's somebody to see you. Right out there on the back verandah. Been waiting for you."

"With a gun, eh?" sneered Jimmy Geary.

## II
## "THE AMBUSH"

BUT THE WHISKEY HAD HIT THROUGH HIS BLOOD, AND the sour fume of it was in his nose and his brain. He had eaten nothing since morning. So the danger of guns meant little to the vastness of his gloom, with this red fire blowing up in it. He knocked the rear door of the bar open. Three men were playing poker at the table that was placed most clearly in his memory. A pair of them had dark faces.

"Take a hand, brother?" said this man cheerfully.

"I've got nothing but chicken feed," said Jimmy.

"Yeah? All we're spending is time."

"I'll be back, then."

He stepped onto the rear verandah, letting the screen door bang behind him. A woman got up from a chair and came slowly toward him. As she moved through the light that slanted out of a window, he recognized Juanita Allen. She was the half-breed daughter of Mac Allen.

"Hello, Jimmy," she said. "I heard you were here. I came on over. That all right? I wanted to see you."

119

"And knife me, too, eh?" said Jimmy. "You used to be Tony Spargo's girl, didn't you?"

"Tony Spargo? That's so long ago, I wouldn't remember!"

She put back her head a little and smiled at him with professional ease. True, he had been eight years out of the world, but he knew that gesture. She backed up into the light, and he saw what the years had done to her. Well, the Mexican blood fades fast.

"How do I look, Jimmy?" she said. "Like hell, eh? Come here and let me take a slant at you, too."

She pulled him forward into the light. That would be easy for an accomplice lodged in the dark of the brush.

"My God, the time's only made a man of you," said Juanita. "But look how it's socked me eight times in the face. You remember, Jimmy? I'm just your age. My birthday comes on Monday before yours. Take a look and tell me what I'm good for now, will you?"

There were some straight lines up and down on her lip. Her smile pulled her face all out of shape and let him see the blanched whiteness of some false teeth. And soap and water would never help her; there was grime in her soul.

"You don't have to tell me. . . I'll tell you. . . I'm done," said Juanita. "I don't mind about the men. To hell with them! But I can't even get a job slinging hash. You'd think I might get a finger in the soup, or something. I'm not good enough for the people around here. Listen to me, Jimmy."

"Yeah. All right. I'm listening," said Jimmy. "Quit crying, will you? I like you fine, Juanita. Please don't cry."

"Take hold of my arm," she said.

He could feel the two bones of the forearm.

"Look at," said Juanita. "I'm sunk. . . I'm done. I've gotta get a break or something, and pull out of here. Jimmy, you were always a good kid. Give me a break, will you?

"I'll give you a break," he heard himself say. "Will you quit crying, Juanita, please? I'm going to give you a break. What d'you need?"

She stopped the crying and started gasping, which was worse. She held him by the wrists with shuddering hands. "I wouldn't need much. There's a little bill over at the boarding house. It's only forty dollars, Jimmy. They'd sock me in jail, if I didn't pay that. And then a little bit more. Car fare, some place. Jimmy, you were always kind. I was sorry, when they slammed you for those three crooks. I knew Tony was a crook. He was a dirty crook to me, too. You see how it is, Jimmy. I wouldn't need the money, if only. . . ."

"You wait here," said Jimmy Geary. "I'm coming back."

She kept a grip on him all the way across the verandah. "I'm going to wait right out here for you," she kept saying. "I'll be expecting you back. I'll wait right here. . . if it takes you all night, I'll be waiting right here."

He got away through the outside door and up the stairs to Number Seventeen. When he got inside, he wanted a drink.

"Hey, Al!" he said to the snorer. He lighted a lamp. Electricity had not been brought out to Graham's Tavern.

"Yeah?" said Alton, turning on the bed. "What time is it?"

"Time for a drink. Where's your flask?"

"Under the pillow."

Jimmy put his hand under and found a gun. Then he found the flask and pulled it out. He unscrewed the top, poured a long shot down his throat. The whiskey horrors choked him. He took another drink to kill them and put the flask down.

"Want some?" he panted.

"Not till I eat."

"Got any money?"

Doc sat up, suddenly. "Yeah, sure," he said. "Sure I've got some money. Help yourself."

He pulled out a wallet. Alton's wallet was always full. Now the bills were packed into a tight sheaf. He pulled out some fifties. There were seven of them. "Three hundred and fifty," he said.

"Sure, kid, sure," said Doc. "Take some more. Take all you want." He took two more.

"A lot of dirty bums is all I've been able to find since you stepped out of the picture," said Alton. "A lot of dirty, yellow-faced rats. You and me will burn up the highway, kid."

Jimmy looked down from the long mustaches of Doc and saw the face of the warden in the shadows at his feet. He saw the prison yard, and the pale eyes of Barney Vane, the lifer who was head trusty. Even the best warden in the world has to use trusties, and a trusty is, you know what. So Jimmy reached for the flask and unscrewed the top of it again.

"You sure you want that?" asked Doc.

"Aw, shut up," said Jimmy, and drank.

"Sure," said Doc Alton. "I'll get on my boots. I'll be waiting for you, while you spend that stuff. I suppose that's what you want to do?"

Jimmy said nothing. He got out of the room and down to the back verandah. He heard the girl rise—the

122

whisper of her clothing and the sound of her drawn breath, but she kept back against the wall. He went to her and stood over her, looking down at her.

"Aw, Jimmy," she moaned suddenly. "Don't say you couldn't get anything. Don't turn me down flat. I swear to God, I haven't eaten. I'm hungry. Give me the price of a square meal, will you, Jimmy?"

"Here, here," said Jimmy Geary. "I've got enough for you. Where's that bag? Here, open it. There's three hundred and fifty in that bag, now. You pay the damned board bill and get out to a better part of the world. This is the rottenest part of creation. Nobody can go straight here."

Juanita caught her breath, started to laugh, choked, sobbed, and then uttered a queer screaming sound that was sob and laughter in one. She wobbled like a hopeless drunk, staggering with hysterics. Well, a man can't very well handle a thing like that. He took her down to the kitchen door and threw it open. Kate was inside drying dishes that a big Negress was washing and putting out on the drain.

"Here, Kate," said Jimmy Geary. "Juanita's hysterical. Get her a drink or something. Quiet her down, will you?"

The face of Kate Graham smiled, as stone might smile. The Negress turned slowly and put her chin up into the air. "That thing!" she said.

Jimmy wanted to kill Kate Graham. Instead, he took Juanita across the room to her and caught her by the wrist and shook her arm.

"You. . . take this girl. . . and be good to her! Haven't you got any more heart than a toad? Take her. . . now. . . and let me see you!"

Kate, with a look of fear and wonder, took that

123

weeping burden in her arms. Jimmy got out of the room onto the verandah. He leaned against a pillar there for a moment, and the stars wavered a little in the sky. Afterward, he went up to Seventeen and found Doc Alton pulling on his second boot.

"Ready, old son?" asked Doc, smiling till his mustaches spread out thin.

Jimmy lifted the pillow, took the gun, and passed it out of view under his coat. "Wait here a while," he said, and went down again. He would play a round or two of that poker, as he had promised to do, for that would show whether or not luck intended to favor him in the old ways.

The three were not impatient. Instead, they greeted him with three different sorts of smiling, so that he had a very odd and vivid feeling that he had known them before. They opened with a round of jackpots, the man with the lofty brow dealing. The Mexican had openers. Jimmy held up a pair of nines and drew another. He won that pot and six dollars, but it wasn't the money that made him feel better and better. He had a genuine kindness for these strangers.

"I haven't met you people before, have I?" he asked.

They had not had that luck, they said.

"I've taken on a little liquor," apologized Jimmy. "You know how it is."

They knew how it was, and it was all right. Two more hands went by before the dark-faced, handsome fellow opposite Jimmy got up, revealing the bullet hole in the wall. He said they ought to have a bit of music, so he wound up the squeaking phonograph and put on a disk. The very first bars of the tune poured the consciousness of Jimmy far into the past.

"You know," he said, when the fellow with the big

black eyes sat down, "it seems as though I've been right here before, with all of you. It's a queer feeling."

The three exchanged glances quietly, and Jimmy made sure that he was quite drunk. If that were the case, he ought not to be sitting in at a poker game, but the music from the scratched and cracked old record on the phonograph held him fascinated, not because it was pleasant but because it hurt like the ache of old wounds.

It was like air-hunger, the sickness of Jimmy. It was like wakening from a nightmare with the vision gone but the fear remaining. He could feel the eyes of the three on him. The game ought to go on, of course, but they seemed to understand a mystery that was closed to him, and they remained half smiling, watchful.

Jimmy looked up, not out of the past but deeper into it. Time closed like water over his head. He leaned a bit forward, and the three leaned the same trifle toward him. They were not smiling, now—not with their eyes, at least.

The music went on. It thrust a knife pain into his right shoulder, into his heart, although he was not following the words just then.

He pointed with his forefinger. "You're Oñate's brother!" he said to the Mexican.

The man nodded and smiled like a Chinese idol.

"You're the brother of Tony Spargo!" said Jimmy Geary to the man across the table.

"I'm his kid brother," sneered Spargo.

"And you're the brother of Gus Warren?"

"Sorry. I'm only his cousin. But maybe I'll do to fill out the hand?"

"Aye," said Jimmy Geary, "you make the three of a kind."

The needle was scratching with every whirl of the

125

disk, and, yet, Jimmy wanted the record to continue endlessly, for he knew that he was to die before the song ended. Spargo had out a gun and laid it on the edge of the table, leaning so far forward that Jimmy could see, over his shoulder, the hole in the wall. He had an insane feeling that his own soul would be drawn through that same gap in the wall and whistled away into nothingness. There would be nothing in the way of an inquiry, even, for the gun of Doc Alton would be found on him. Perhaps that was Alton's part in the plot—to see that the victim went heeled to the fight. But there would be no fight. The music poured icy sleep over his hands.

They were going to get him on the down strain of that weary sing-song. He could see the murder tightening in the hand and the eyes of Spargo. Then Kate Graham spoke out of the doorway, deliberately, as though she did not realize that the song was running swiftly to its end: "The thing's off. He hasn't got a gun. It's murder, if you turn loose on him. . . and I'll give the testimony to hang you."

The Mexican uttered a little soft, musical cry of pain. Spargo's lips kept stretching thinner over his teeth. He said the words through Jimmy to the girl: "Are you gonna be the blonde rat? Are you gonna run out?"

"You fixed this job and got us here!" cried the cousin of Gus Warren. "Now what's the idea?"

"Look!" moaned Oñate. "I have the same knife for him. Look, *señorita!* It is the same!"

"What did I care about your brother, Oñate?" asked the girl calmly. "Or about four-flushing Gus Warren? And I've just been getting some news about Tony Spargo. It made me send for the sheriff. Are you three going to be here to shake hands with him?"

126

They were not going to be there. They stood up, with young Spargo running the tips of his fingers absently over the bullet hole in the wall. They all looked at Kate as they went out, but they said nothing to her.

That silence continued in the room until after the first pounding and then the departing ripple of the hoofbeats. Jimmy stood up.

"The sheriff's not coming, if that's what you mean," said the girl.

"Sit down here," said Jimmy. The whiskey was gone. Inside him there was only emptiness, with a throb in it.

"There's no good talking," said the girl, but she came to the table and slipped into the chair where Tony Spargo had once sat. She was only calm from a distance. At close hand he could see the tremor as he leaned across the table.

"You were only a kid," said Jimmy. "That's what I don't understand."

The song had ended; the needle was scratching steadily in the last groove. A nick in the disk struck the needle point at greater and still greater intervals.

"It was Tony Spargo, was it?" said Jimmy.

"I was nearly sixteen," she said. "He used to talk to me and look at me with his greasy eyes. I never saw the grease in them until this evening. I didn't know till after she'd talked to me." She folded her hands. The fingers were smooth and slender. She wore rubber gloves around the kitchen and that was why. But in spite of her double grip, the hands would not stop quivering.

"What are you afraid of?" asked Jimmy.

"You know what I'm afraid of. You're going to say something. Go on and say it and get it over with. I can take that, too."

"Hello," said the voice of Doc Alton from the

doorway.

"Go on away, Doc," said Jimmy. "Wait a minute, though. Come and take this."

He kept holding the girl with his eyes as he held out the gun to the side. Doc Alton took it.

"I owe you some money," said Jimmy Geary, "and I'm going to keep on owing it for a while."

"That's all right," said Doc Alton. "Are you. . . are you staying around here, Jimmy?"

The mournful wistfulness of his voice left Jimmy untouched.

"I'm staying around here," he answered. "So long, Doc."

Doc Alton went out.

"I mean," said Jimmy, "I'm staying around unless you say no."

She drew in a breath and closed her eyes. "Wait a minute," she whispered. "In a minute. . . I'll be able to talk."

He knew that, if he put his hand over hers, he would stop their trembling, but he sat up straight and waited. The needle bumped for the last time on the disk and the scratching ended. Another sound rose and moved forward in Jimmy, a rushing and singing like wind or like mountain waters that go on forever.

# DEATH IN ALKALI FLAT

*This novelette has a complex history. Originally printed as "Sun and Sand" in the February 16, 1935 issue of* **Western Story Magazine** *under the Hugh Owen byline, it was never meant to appear in a Street & Smith pulp. The story was purchased by Frank Blackwell—at Faust's lowest rate of two cents a word—only after the Western pulp,* **Mavericks**, *expired at the end of 1934. Obviously, "Death in Alkali Flat," as Faust had titled it, would have been printed in* **Mavericks** *as the fifth and final story in Max Brand's Sleeper series had the magazine survived. By 1935 Faust was no longer writing for Street & Smith. In fact, after this one, only one other Faust entry appeared in* **Western Story Magazine**, *the short "Eagles Over Crooked Creek"— printed in 1938, but written in November of 1935 for another market. After Blackwell had purchased "Death in Alkali Flat" by rebound, he faced a problem. The hero was a semi-tramp known as Sleeper. He rode a golden stallion named Careless and was working off a debt to a bald, pockmarked peddler named Pop Lowry. All of these had been featured in the four previous issues of* **Mavericks**. *The story had to be separated from its association with the earlier stories. Solution: change the names. Thus, Sleeper, the semi-tramp, became Jigger. Careless, the golden stallion, became Fanfare. Pop Lowry, the peddler, became Doc Landy. With the names of the characters restored for this edition, "Death in Alkali Flat" is a perfect example of Faust's remarkable ability to draw the reader deeply into his narrative so that he or she experiences the dry thirst,* *the burning sun, and the sense of hopeless exhaustion as they share these trials with the story's hero.*

# I
## "SILVER SNAKE"

AT THE PAWNBROKER'S WINDOW, SLEEPER DISMOUNTED. He had only a few dollars in his pocket, but he had an almost childish weakness for bright things, and he could take pleasure with his eyes even when he could not buy his fancy. But on account of the peculiar slant of the sun, the only thing he could see clearly, at first, was his own image. The darkness of his skin startled him. It was no wonder that some people took him for a Gypsy or an Indian. He was dressed like a Gypsy vagrant, too, with a great patch on one shoulder of his shirt and one sleeve terminating in tatters at the elbow. However, he was not one to pride himself on appearance. He stretched himself; his dark eyes closed in the completeness of his yawn. Then he pressed his face closer to the window to make out what was offered for sale.

There were trays of rings, stick pins, jeweled cuff links. There were four pairs of pearl-handled revolvers; some hatbands of Mexican wheelwork done in metal; a little heap of curiously worked *conchos*; a number of watches, silver or gold; knives; some fine lace, yellow with age; a silver tea set—who had ever drunk tea in the mid-afternoon in this part of the world?—an odd bit of Mexican featherwork; spurs of plain steel, silver, or gold; and a host of odds and ends of all sorts.

The eye of Sleeper, for all his apparently lazy deliberation, moved a little more swiftly than the snapping end of a whiplash. After a glance, he had seen this host of entangled curiosities so well that he would

130

have been able to list and describe most of them. He had settled his glance on one oddity that amused him—a key ring which was a silver snake that turned on itself in a double coil and gripped its tail in its mouth, while it stared at the world and at Sleeper with glittering little eyes of green.

Sleeper went to the door, and the great golden stallion from which he had dismounted started to follow. So he lifted a finger and stopped the horse with that small sign, then he entered.

The pawnbroker was a foreigner—he might have been anything from a German to an Armenian, and he had a divided beard that descended in two points, gray and jagged as rock. He had a yellow, wrinkled forehead, and his thick glasses made two glimmering obscurities of his eyes. When Sleeper asked to see the silver snake key ring, the bearded man took up the tray that contained it.

"How much?" asked Sleeper.

"Ten dollars," said the pawnbroker.

"Ten which?" asked Sleeper.

"With emeralds for eyes, too. But I make it seven-fifty for such a young man."

Sleeper did not know jewels, but he knew men.

"I'll give you two and a half," he said.

"I sell things," answered the pawnbroker. "I can't afford to give them away."

"Good bye, brother," said Sleeper, but he had seen a shimmer of doubt in the eyes of the other, and he was not surprised to be called back from the door.

"Well," said the pawnbroker, "I've only had it in my window for two or three hours. . . it's good luck to make a quick sale, so here you are."

As Sleeper laid the money on the counter, he

commenced to twist off the keys.

"Hold on," said Sleeper. "Let the tassels stay on it, too. They make it look better."

"You want to mix them up with your own keys?" asked the pawnbroker.

"I haven't any keys of my own," said Sleeper, laughing, and went from the pawnshop at once.

As he walked down the street, the stallion followed him, trailing a little distance to the rear, and people turned to look at the odd sight, for the horse looked fit for a king, and Sleeper was in rags. There were plenty of men in the streets of Tucker Flat, because, since the bank robbery of three months ago, the big mines of the town had been shutting down one by one. They never had paid very much more than the cost of production, and the quarter million stolen from the Levison Bank had consisted chiefly of their deposits. Against that blow the three mines had struggled, but failed to recover. The result was that a flood of laborers was set adrift. Some of them had gone off through the mountains in a vain quest for new jobs; others loitered about Tucker Flat in the hope that something would happen to reopen the mines. That was why the sheriff had his hands full. Tucker Flat always was as hard as nails, but now it was harder still.

The streets were full, but the saloons were empty, as Sleeper soon observed when he went into one for a glass of beer. He sat at the darkest corner table, nursing the drink and his gloomy thoughts. Pop Lowry had appointed this town and this evening as the moment for their meeting, and only the devil that lived in the brain of the pseudo-peddler could tell what new and dangerous task Lowry would name for Sleeper.

He had been an hour in the shadows, staring at his

thoughts, before the double swing doors of the saloon were pushed open by a man who looked over the interior with a quick eye, then muttered: "Let's try the red-eye in here, old son."

With a companion, he sauntered toward the bar. Sleeper was at once completely awake. For that exploring glance which the stranger had cast around the room had not been merely to survey the saloon, it had been in quest of a face, and, when his eye had lighted on Sleeper, he had come in at once.

But what could Sleeper be to him? Sleeper had never seen him before. In the great spaces of his memory, where faces appeared more thickly than whirling leaves, never once had he laid eyes on either of the pair. The first man was tall, meager, with a crooked neck and a projecting Adam's apple. The skin was fitted tightly over the bones of his face; his hair was blond, his eyebrows very white, and his skin sun-blackened. It was altogether a face that would not be forgotten easily. The second fellow was an opposite type, fat, dark, with immense power swelling the shoulders and sleeves of his shirt.

The two looked perfectly the parts of cowpunchers; certainly they had spent their lives in the open. There was nothing to catch the eyes about them as extraordinary except that both wore their guns well down the thigh, so that the handles of them were conveniently in grasp of the finger tips.

Having spent half a second glancing at them, Sleeper spent the next moments in carefully analyzing the two. Certainly he never had seen their faces. He never had heard their names—from their talk he learned that the tall fellow was Tim, and the shorter man was called Buzz. They looked the part of cowpunchers, perfectly,

133

except that the palms of their hands did not seem to be thickened or callused.

What could they want with Sleeper, unless they had been sent to the town of Tucker Flat in order to locate Sleeper and relay to him orders from Pop Lowry?

Several more men came into the saloon. It was apparent that they had nothing to do with the first couple. However, a few moments later both Buzz and Tim were seated at a table with two more. By the very way that tall Tim shuffled the cards, it was clear to Sleeper that these fellows probably had easier ways of making money than working for it.

Hands uncallused; guns worn efficiently although uncomfortably low—these were small indications, but they were enough to make Sleeper suspicious. The two looked to him more and more like a couple of Lowry's lawbreakers.

"How about you, stranger?" said Tim, nodding at Sleeper. "Make a fifth at poker?"

"I've only got a few bucks on me," said Sleeper. "But I'll sit in, if you want."

He could have sworn that this game had been arranged by Tim and Buzz solely for the purpose of drawing him into it. Yet, everything had been done very naturally.

He remained out for the first three hands, then, on three queens, he pulled in a jackpot. Half an hour later he was betting his last penny. He lost it at once.

"You got a nice spot of bad luck," said Buzz Mahoney, who was mixing the cards at the moment. "But stick with the game. If you're busted, we'll lend you something."

"I've got nothing worth a loan," said Sleeper.

"Haven't you got a gun tucked away, somewhere?"

134

"No. No gun."

He saw a thin gleam of wonder and satisfaction commingled in the eyes of Tim Riley.

"Empty out your pockets, " said Tim. "Maybe you've got a picture of your best girl. I'll lend you something on that."

He laughed as he spoke. They all laughed. Sleeper obediently put the contents of his pockets on the table, a jumble of odds and ends.

"All right," said Tim at once. "Lend you ten bucks on that, brother."

Ten dollars? The whole lot was not worth five, new. But Sleeper accepted the money. He accepted and lost it all by an apparently foolish bet in the next hand. But he wanted to test the strangers at once.

"I'm through, boys," he said, and pushed back his chair.

He was eager to see if they would still persuade him to remain in the game. But not a word was said, except that Buzz Mahoney muttered: "Your bad luck is a regular long streak, today. Sorry to lose you, kid."

Sleeper laughed a little, pushing in his cards with a hand that lingered on them for just an instant.

In that moment he had found what he expected—a little, almost microscopic smudge that was not quite true to the regular pattern on the backs of the cards. It was a tiny thing, but the eye of Sleeper was a little sharper than that of a hawk which turns its head in the middle sky and sees in the dim forest of the grass below the scamper of a little field mouse.

The cards were marked. Mahoney or Tim Riley had done that. They were marked for the distinct purpose of beating Sleeper, for the definite end of getting away something that had been in his possession.

135

What was it that they had wanted so much? What was it that had brought them on his trail?

## II
## "A NEW JOB"

IT WAS PITCH DARK WHEN POP LOWRY REACHED THE deserted shack outside the town of Tucker Flat. He whistled once and again, and, when he received no answer, he began to curse heavily. In the darkness, with the swift surety of long practice, he stripped the packs from the mules, hobbled and side-lined them. Presently they were sucking up water noisily at the little rivulet that crossed the clearing.

The peddler, in the meantime, had kindled a small fire in the open fireplace which stood before the shack, and he soon had the flames rising, as he laid out his cooking pans and provisions. This light struck upward on his long jaw and heavy nose, merely glinting across the baldness of his head and the silver pockmarks that were littered over his features. When he turned, reaching here and there with his long arms, the huge, deformed bunch behind his shoulders loomed. It was rather a camel's hump of strength than a deformity of the spine.

Bacon began to hiss in the pan. Coffee bubbled in the pot. Potatoes were browning in the coals beside the fire. Soft pone steamed in its baking pan. Now the peddler set out a tin of plum jam and prepared to begin his feast. It was at this moment that he heard a yawn, or what seemed a yawn, on the farther side of the clearing.

The big hands of the peddler instantly were holding a shotgun in readiness. Peering through the shadows, on the very margin of his firelight he made out a dim patch of gold, then the glow of big eyes, and, at last, he was aware of a big horse lying motionless on the ground, while close to him, his head and shoulders comfortably pillowed on a hummock, appeared Sleeper.

"Sleeper!" yelled the peddler. "You been here all the time? Didn't you hear the whistle?"

"Why should I show up before eating time?" asked Sleeper.

He stood up and stretched himself. The stallion began to rise, also, but a gesture from the master made it sink to the ground again.

"I dunno why I should feed a gent too lazy to help me take off those packs and cook the meal," growled Pop Lowry. He thrust out his jaw in an excess of malice.

"You want to feed me because you always feed the hungry," said Sleeper. "Because the bigness of old Pop's heart is one of the things that everyone talks about. A rough diamond, but a heart of gold. A. . . ."

"The devil with the people, and you, too," said Pop.

He looked on gloomily while Sleeper, uninvited, helped himself to food and commenced to eat.

"Nothing but brown sugar for this coffee?" demanded Sleeper.

"It's too good for you, even that way," answered Pop. "What makes you so hungry?"

"Because I didn't eat since noon."

"Why not? There's all the food in the world in Tucker Flat."

"Broke," said Sleeper.

"Broke? How can you be broke, when I gave you fifteen hundred dollars two weeks ago?" shouted Pop.

"Well," said Sleeper, "the fact is that faro parted me from five hundred."

"Faro? You fool!" said Pop. "But that still left a whole thousand. . . and, from the looks of you, you

137

didn't spend anything on clothes."

"I ran into Jeff Beacon, and old Jeff was flat."

"How much did you give him?"

"I don't know. I gave him the roll, and he took a part of it."

"You don't know how much?"

"I forgot to count it, afterward."

"Are you clean crazy, Sleeper?"

"Jeff needed money worse than I did. A man with a family to take care of needs a lot of money, Pop."

"Still, that left you several hundred. What happened to it?"

"I met Steve Walters when he was feeling lucky, and I staked him for poker."

"What did his luck turn into?"

"Wonderful, Pop. He piled up nearly two thousand in an hour."

"Where was your share of it?"

"Why, Steve hit three bad hands and plunged, and he was taken to the cleaners. So I gave him something to eat on and rode away." Sleeper added: "When today came along, somehow I had only a few dollars in my pocket."

"I'd rather pour water on the desert than put money in your pocket!" shouted Pop Lowry. "It ain't human, the way you throw it away."

He continued to glare for a moment and growl. He was still shaking his head as he commenced champing his food.

"You didn't even have a price of a meal?" he demanded at last.

"That's quite a story."

"I don't want to hear it," snapped Pop Lowry. "I've got a job for you."

"I've just finished a job for you," said Sleeper.

"What of it?" demanded Pop Lowry. "You signed up to do what I pleased for three months, didn't you?"

"I did," sighed Sleeper. He thought regretfully of the impulse that had led him into putting himself at the beck and call of this old vulture. But his word had been given.

"And there's more than two months of that time left, ain't there?"

"I suppose so."

"Then listen to me, while I tell you what I want you to do."

"Wait till you hear my story."

"Rats with your story. I don't want to hear it."

"Oh, you'll want to hear it all right."

"What makes you think so?" asked the peddler.

"Because you like one thing even more than money."

"What do I like more?"

"Trouble," said Sleeper. "You love it like the rat that you are."

In fact, as the peddler thrust out his jaw and wrinkled his eyes, he looked very like a vast rodent. He overlooked the insult to ask: "What sort of trouble?"

"Something queer. I told you I was broke today. That's because I lost my last few dollars playing poker. I played the poker because I *wanted* to lose."

"Wanted?" echoed Pop Lowry. "That's too crazy even for you. I don't believe it."

"I'll tell you how it was. I was sitting with a glass of beer, when two *hombres* walked into the saloon. . . by the look they gave me, I knew they were on my trail. . . and I wondered why, because I'd never seen them before. I let them get me into a poker game and take my cash. I knew that wasn't what they wanted. When I was frozen out, they were keen to lend me a stake and got me to empty my pockets on the table. I put a handful of junk on the table, and they loaned me ten dollars, and I let that go in the next hand. They didn't offer to stake me again. They wanted something that was in my pockets. When they got that, they were satisfied. Now, then, what was it that they were after?"

"What did they look like?" asked Pop Lowry.

"Anything up to murder," said Sleeper promptly.

"What was the stuff you put on the table?"

"Half a pack of wheat-straw papers, a full sack of tobacco, a penknife with one blade broken, a twist of twine, sulphur matches, a leather wallet with nothing in it except a letter from a girl, a key ring and some keys, a handkerchief, a pocket comb in a leather case, a stub of a pencil. That was all."

"The letter from the girl. What girl?" asked Lowry.

"None of your business," said Sleeper.

"It may have been *their* business, though."

"Not likely. Her name wasn't signed to the letter, anyway. She didn't say anything, except talk about the weather. Nobody could have made anything of that letter."

"Any marks on the wallet?"

"None that mattered, so far as I know."

"I've seen you write notes on cigarette papers."

"No notes on those."

"What were you doing with a key ring and keys? You don't own anything with locks on it."

"Caught my eye in the pawnshop today. Little silver snake with green eyes."

"Anything queer about that snake?"

"Good Mexican work. That's all."

"The letter's the answer," said Pop Lowry. "There

140

was something in that letter."

"They're welcome to it."

"Or in the keys. What sort of keys?"

"Three for padlocks, two regular door keys, something that looked like a skeleton, and a little flat key of white metal."

"Any marks on those keys?"

"Only on the little one. The number on it was one two six five."

"You've got an eye," said Pop Lowry. "When I think what an eye and a brain and a hand you've got, it sort of makes me sick. Nothin' in the world that you couldn't do, if you weren't so dog-gone honest."

Sleeper did not answer. He was brooding, and now he said: "Could have been the keys? I didn't think of that." Then he added: "It *was* the keys!"

"How d'you know?" asked Pop.

"I remember now that, when I bought them, the pawnbroker said that he had just put the ring out for sale a couple of hours before."

"Ha!" grunted Pop. "You mean that the two gents had gone back to the pawnshop to redeem the key ring?"

"Why not? Maybe they'd come a long way to redeem that key ring. Maybe the time was up yesterday. They found the thing gone. . . they got my description. . . they trailed me. . . they worked the stuff out of my pockets onto the table. . . and there you are! Pop, they were headed for some sort of dirty work. . . something big."

Pop Lowry began to sweat. He forgot to drink his coffee.

"We'll forget the other job I was going to give you," he said. "Maybe there ain't a bean in this, but we'll run it down."

"I knew you'd smell the poison in the air and like it,"

141

said Sleeper, grinning.

"What would put you on their trail? What would the number on that little key mean?"

"Hotel room? No, it wasn't big enough for that. It couldn't mean anything. . . in this part of the world. . . except a post office box. No other lock would be shallow enough for it to fit."

"There's an idea!" exclaimed Pop Lowry. "That's a big number. . . one two six five. Take a big town to have that many post office boxes."

"Weldon is the only town big enough for that. . . the only town inside of three hundred miles."

"That pair is traveling for Weldon," agreed Lowry. "They wanted that bunch of keys. Get 'em, Sleeper! That's your job. Just get those keys and find out what they're to open. And start now!"

## III
## "IN WELDON PASS"

BUZZ MAHONEY, OPENING THE DOOR OF HIS ROOM at the hotel in Tucker Flat, lighted a match to ignite the lamp on the center table. Then he heard a whisper behind him and tried to turn around, but a blow landed accurately at the base of his skull and dropped him down a well of darkness. Sleeper, leaning over him, unhurried, lighted another match, and, fumbling through the pockets, found almost at once the silver snake key ring. Then he descended to the street, using a back window, instead of the lobby and the front door. Before he had gone half a block, he heard stamping and shouting in the hotel, and knew that his victim had recovered and was trying to discover the source of his fall.

Sleeper, pausing near the first streak of lamplight that shone through a window, examined the keys with a swift glance. There had been seven keys before; there were only six now. That was what sent Sleeper swiftly around the corner to the place where Pop Lowry waited for him.

"I've got them," he said, "but the one for the post office box is gone. Mahoney had the rest. . . but Tim Riley is gone with the little key."

"There's something in that post office box," answered Pop. "Go and get it."

"He's got a head start," answered Sleeper.

"He's got a head start, but you've got your horse, and, if Careless can't make up the lost ground, nothing can. Ride for Weldon and try to catch Tim Riley on the way. I'm heading straight on for Weldon myself. I'll get there sometime tomorrow. Quit the trails and head straight for Weldon Pass. You'll catch your bird there."

Sleeper sat on his heels and closed his eyes. He was seeing in his mind all the details of the ground over which he would have to travel, if he wished to take a short cut to Weldon Pass. Then he stood up, nodded, and stretched again.

"I'll run along," he said.

"Have another spot of money?" asked the peddler.

He took out fifty dollars, counted it with a grudging hand from his wallet, and passed it to Sleeper, who received it without thanks.

"How long before somebody cuts your gizzard open to get your money, Pop?"

"That's what salts the meat and makes the game worthwhile," said Pop Lowry. "Never knowing whether I'm gonna wake up, when I go to sleep at night."

"How many murders do you dream about, Pop?"

143

pursued Sleeper casually.

"I got enough people in my dreams," said Pop Lowry, grinning. "And some of 'em keep on talking after I know they're dead. But my conscience don't bother me none. I ain't such a fool, Sleeper."

Sleeper turned on his heel without answer or farewell. Five minutes later he was traveling toward Weldon Pass on the back of the stallion.

If Tim Riley had in fact started so long ahead of him toward the town of Weldon, it would take brisk travel to catch him in the narrow throat of the pass, so Sleeper laid out an air line and traveled it as straight as a bird. There were ups and downs which ordinary men on ordinary horses never would have attempted. Sleeper was on his feet half the time, climbing rugged slopes up which the stallion followed him like a great cat. Or again Sleeper worked his way down some perilous steep with the golden horse scampering and sliding to the rear, always with his nose close to the ground to study the exact places where his master had stepped. For the man knew exactly what the horse could do, and never took him over places too slippery or too abrupt for him to cover. In this work they gave the impression of two friends struggling toward a common end, rather than of master and servant.

So they came out on a height above Weldon Pass, and, looking down on it, Sleeper saw the moon break through clouds and gild the pass with light. It was a wild place, with scatterings of hardy brush here and there, even an occasional tree, but on the whole it looked like a junk heap of stone with a course kicked through the center of it. Rain had been falling recently. The whole pass was bright with water, and it was against the thin gleam of this background that Sleeper saw the small

144

shadow of the other rider coming toward him. He went down the last abrupt slope at once to intercept the course of the other rider.

He was hardly at the bottom before he could hear the faint clinking sounds made by the hoofs of the approaching horse. A whisper made the stallion sink from view behind some small boulders. Sleeper himself ran up to the top of a boulder half the size of a house, and crouched there. He could see the stranger coming, the head of the horse nodding up and down in the pale moonlight. Sleeper tied a bandanna around the lower part of his face.

Ten steps from Sleeper's waiting place, he made sure that it was tall Tim Riley in person, for there Riley stopped his horse and let it drink from a little freshet that ran across the narrow floor of the ravine. It was a magnificent horse that he rode—over sixteen hands, sloping shoulders, high withers, big bones, well-let-down hocks, and flat knees. *A horse too good for a working cowpuncher to have*, thought Sleeper. And his last doubt about the character of Tim Riley disappeared. The man was a crooked card played with a crooked companion; he was probably a criminal in other ways, as well. Men are not apt to make honest journeys through the middle of the night and over places as wild as the Weldon Pass.

When the horse had finished drinking, Riley rode on again. He was passing the boulder that sheltered Sleeper, when his mount stopped suddenly and threw up its head with a snort. Riley, with the speed of an automatic reaction, snatched out a gun. There was a well-oiled ease in the movement, a professional touch of grace that did not escape the eye of Sleeper. He could only take his man half by surprise, now, but he rose

145

from behind his rampart of rock and leaped headlong.

He sprang from behind, yet the flying shadow of danger seemed to pass over the brain of Riley. He jerked his head and gun around while Sleeper was still in the air, then Sleeper struck him with the full lunging weight of his body, and they rolled together from the back of the horse.

The gun had exploded once, while they were in the air. Sleeper remained unscathed. Now he found himself fighting for his life against an enemy as strong and swift and fierce as a mountain lion.

A hundred times Sleeper had fought with his hands, but always victory had been easy. The ancient science of *jujitsu*, that he had spent patient years learning, gave him a vast advantage in spite of his slender bulk. He had struggled with great two-hundred-pounders who were hardened fighting men, but always it was like the battle between the meager wasp and the huge, powerful tarantula. The spider fights with blind strength, laying hold with its steel shears wherever it can; the wasp drives its poisoned sting at the nerve centers.

That is the art of *jujitsu*. At the pits of the arms or the side of the neck or the back, or inside the legs or in the pit of the stomach, there are places where the great nerves come close to the surface, vulnerable to a hard pressure or a sharp blow. Sleeper knew those spots as an anatomist might know them. Men who fought him were rarely hurt unless they hurled their own weight at him too blindly, for half the great art of *jujitsu* lies in using the strength of the antagonist against him. Usually the victim of Sleeper recovered as from a trance, with certain vaguely tingling pains still coursing through parts of his body. But not a bone would be broken, and the bruises were few.

146

He tried all his art now, and he found that art checked and baffled at every turn. Tall and spare of body, Tim Riley looked almost fragile, but from the first touch Sleeper found him a creature of whalebone and Indian rubber. Every fiber of Riley's body was a strong wire, and in addition he was an expert wrestler. Before they had rolled twice on the ground, Sleeper was struggling desperately in the defense. Then the arm of Riley caught him with a frightful strangle hold that threatened to break his neck before it choked him. Suddenly Sleeper lay still.

Tim Riley seemed to sense surrender in this yielding, this sudden pulpiness of body and muscle. Instead of offering quarter, Riley began to snarl like a dog that has sunk its teeth in a death grip. He kept jerking the crook of his arm deeper and deeper into the throat of Sleeper, who lay inert, face down. Flames and smoke seemed to shoot upward through Sleeper's brain, but in that instant of relaxation he had gathered his strength and decided on his counterstroke.

He twisted his right leg outside that of his enemy, raised the foot until with his heel he located the knee of Riley, then kicked the sharp heel heavily against the inside of the joint. Tim Riley yelled with agony. The blow fell again, and he twisted his body frantically away from the torture. That movement gave Sleeper his chance, and with the sharp edge of the palm, hardened almost like wood by long practice in the trick, he struck the upper arm of Riley.

It loosened its grip like a numb, dead thing. With his other arm Riley tried to get the same fatal hold, but Sleeper had twisted like a writhing snake. He struck again with the edge of the palm, and the blow fell like the stroke of a blunt cleaver across the million nerves that run up the side of the neck. The head of Riley fell over as though an axe had struck deep. He lay not motionless but vaguely stirring, making a groaning, wordless complaint.

Sleeper, in a moment, had trussed him like a bird for market. Still the wits had not fully returned to Riley as Sleeper rifled his pockets. But he found not a sign of the little flat, white key that had the number 1265 stamped upon it. He crumpled the clothes of the man, feeling that such a small object might have been hidden in a seam. Then he pulled off the boots of Riley, and, when he took out the first insole, he found what he wanted. The little key flashed like an eye in the moonlight, then he dropped it into his pocket.

The voice of Tim Riley pleaded from the ground: "You ain't gonna leave me here, brother, are you? And what on earth did you use to hit me? Where did you have it. . . up your sleeve?"

Sleeper leaned and looked into the hard face of the other. Then he muttered: "You'll be all right. People will be riding through the pass in the early morning. So long, partner."

Then he took Riley's horse by the reins and led it away among the rocks toward the place where he had left Careless, the stallion.

## IV
## "THE CHART"

NEITHER ON THE STREETS OF WELDON NOR IN THE post office itself did people pay much attention to Sleeper because the Weldon newspaper had published an extra which told that the body of Joe Mendoza, the escaped fugitive from the state prison, had been found.

That news was of sufficient importance to occupy all eyes with reading and all tongues with talk. All it meant to Sleeper was the cover under which he could approach his work.

He went straight into the post office and found there what he had expected in a town of the size of Weldon— a whole wall filled by the little mail boxes, each with a glass insert in the door so that it could be seen if mail were waiting inside. In the right-hand corner, shoulder-high, appeared No. 1265. Inside it, he could see a single thin envelope.

The key fitted at once. The little bolt of the lock slipped with a click, and the door opened. Sleeper took out the envelope and slammed the small door so that the spring lock engaged.

On the envelope was written: Mr. Oliver Badget, Box 1265, Weldon. And in the upper left-hand corner: To be delivered only to Oliver Badget in person.

Ⓥ Ⓥ Ⓥ Ⓥ Ⓥ

The camping places of the peddler in his tours through the mountains were perfectly known to Sleeper. Therefore he was waiting in a wooded hollow just outside of Weldon, when Pop Lowry shambled into the glade later that afternoon.

Pop Lowry shouted an excited greeting, but Sleeper remained flat on his back, his hands cupped under his head while he stared up through the green gloom of a pine tree at the little splashes of blue heaven above. In slanted patches the sun warmed his body.

The peddler, not waiting to pull the pack saddles off his tired mules, stood over Sleeper and stared critically down at him.

149

"That gent Riley was a tough *hombre*, eh? Too tough for you, Sleeper?" he asked.

"I got the key from him," said Sleeper. "There was a box numbered one two six five at the post office, and this was what was inside." He fished the envelope from his pocket and tossed it into the air. The big hand of the peddler darted out and caught the prize. Jerking out the fold of paper that it contained, Pop Lowry stared at a singular pattern. There was not a written word on the soiled sheet; there was only a queer jumble of dots, triangles, and one wavering, crooked line that ran across the paper from one corner to the other. Beside one bend of the wavering line appeared a cross.

"This here is the spot," argued the peddler.

"The cross is the spot," agreed Sleeper. "And a lot that means!"

"The triangles are trees," said Pop.

"Or mountains," answered Sleeper.

"The dots. . . what would they be, kid?"

"How do I know? Cactus. . . rocks. . . I don't know."

"This crooked line is a road, Sleeper."

"Or a valley, or a ravine."

"It's hell!" said Lowry.

He stared at Sleeper, who remained motionless. The wind ruffled his black hair; the blue of his eyes was as still and peaceful as the sky above them. Pop Lowry cursed again and then sat down, cross-legged.

"Put your brains on this here, Sleeper," he said. "Two brains are better than one."

"I've put my brain on it, but you can see for yourself that we'll never make anything out of it."

"Why not?"

"Well, it's simply a chart to stir up the memory of Oliver Badget. Oliver is the boy who knows what those marks mean. Call it a road. . . that crooked line. Well, at the seventh bend from the lower corner of the page, there, along that road, there's something planted. Oliver wants to be able to find it. But where does the road begin? Where does he begin to count the bends?"

"From Weldon," suggested the peddler.

"Yes. Or from a bridge, or a clump of trees, or something like that. And there's twenty roads or trails leading into Weldon."

Pop Lowry groaned. He took out a plug of chewing tobacco, clamped his teeth into a corner of it, and bit off a liberal quid with a single powerful closing of his jaws. He began to masticate the tobacco slowly. "A gent with something on hand wants to put it away," he said, thinking aloud. "He takes and hides it. He hides it in a place so dog-gone mixed up that even he can't be sure that he'll remember. So he leaves a chart. Where's he going to hide the *chart*, though?"

"Where nobody would ever think of looking " agreed Sleeper. "He rents a post office box and puts the chart in an envelope addressed to himself. Nobody else could get that envelope because nobody else has the key, and nobody would call for mail in Badget's name and get the envelope, either. Because that letter would have to be signed for in Badget's signature before the clerk would turn the thing over. But now that he's got the chart hidden, all he has to do is to hide the key. And where would he hide the key? Well, in a place just as public as the post office box, where everybody could see it. So he hocks that key ring and all the keys on it at a pawnshop."

Lowry sighed. "Nobody would go to all of this trouble, Sleeper," he commented, "unless what was hidden out was a dog-gone big pile."

151

"Nobody would," agreed Sleeper.

"Now Mister Badget turns up and tries to get his key, and finds out that his time has just run out. He hurries like the devil to get to that key in time, but he's too late. Sleeper has the key. He gets it away from Sleeper. . . . Why, that all sounds dog-gone reasonable and logical."

"Badget isn't another name for Riley or for Mahoney," declared Sleeper.

"Why not?"

"Well, Badget himself could go to the post office without the key and get the letter any time by signing for it."

"True," agreed Lowry. Then he added, after a moment of thought: "Badget couldn't come himself. He had to send friends to make sure that that key didn't get into the wrong hands. He sent friends to maybe just pay the pawnbroker's loan and renew it. . . and pay for the post office box. Why didn't Badget come himself? Sick? In jail?"

"Or dead," said Sleeper.

"Sleeper, there's something important hidden out where that cross is marked."

"We'll never find it without a key to the chart," said Sleeper. "It's a good little map, all right, but unless we know what part of the country to fit it to, we'll never locate what's under the cross. It may be a district five hundred miles from here, for all we know."

"What'll we do?" asked Pop Lowry.

"Wait, Pop. That's the only good thing that we can do."

"What good will waiting do?"

"The postmaster has a master key for all of those boxes. Well, the postmaster is going to lose that key today or tomorrow. And right afterward, box one two six five is going to be opened."

"There won't be anything in it," protested Lowry. "Whatcha mean, Sleeper?"

"You can copy the chart, and then I'll put the original back in the post office box."

"What happens then? You mean that Riley and Mahoney come along, rob the postmaster of the master key, get the chart, and then start out on the trail with us behind them?"

"With *me* behind them," corrected Sleeper. "I don't need you."

The big peddler swore. "Yeah," he said, "you can disappear like a sand flea and turn up like a wildcat whenever you want to. You'll be able to trail 'em, all right."

Sleeper sighed. "Copy the chart," he said. "I'm going to sleep. Because after I take that envelope back to the post office, I've got to find a place and stay awake day and night to see who goes into that building, and who comes out again."

Lowry, without a word of answer, sat down to his drawing.

## V
## "ALKALI FLAT"

THERE WAS A THREE-STORY HOTEL OPPOSITE THE POST office, and here Sleeper lay at a window night and day for four long days. They were hot, windless days, and he hardly closed his eyes for more than a half hour at a time, but the keenness of his attention never diminished. Over the low shoulders of the post office, from his place of vantage, he could look all around the environs of the building he spied upon. The nights were clear, with moonlight; the days were the more difficult.

He could not tell when Riley or Mahoney would appear in one of the sudden swirls of people who slipped suddenly through the swing doors of the building, disappeared, and came out again a few moments later. It was quite possible that they would attempt to disguise themselves. Even then he would have more than a good chance of identifying them. He had learned long ago to look not only at the face of a man but also at the shape of his head, the angle of nose and forehead, and particularly at any strangeness of contour in the ear. A man may become either thin or fat, but his height is not altered. And the general outline of the head and shoulders, whether the man comes toward the eye or goes from it, may often be recognized. Even so, hawk-eyed as he was, it would be fumbling in the dark—and like a patient fisher he remained waiting. Agonies of impatience he hid away behind a smile.

One cause of his impatience was his desire to finish up the job for Lowry. Pop had helped him in his great need but had expected a three months' servitude in exchange. Sleeper loved danger, and Pop could supply it, but it was unsavory, unclean, and Sleeper liked things as shining clear as the coat of the stallion Careless. His code made him live up to his given word. What he would do to Pop, when his term of service was up, put the only good taste in his mouth in many a day.

It was on the fourth day that tall Pop Lowry stalked into the room and pushed his dusty hat back on his head. The hot reek of the outdoors entered with him.

He said: "Oliver Badget was Joe Mendoza. I just seen a bit of Mendoza's handwriting, so I know. Buzz Mahoney and Tim Riley were the best friends of Joe. Mendoza is dead. Buzz and Tim are carryin' on where

Mendoza left off. That means they're starting something big. So big that Mendoza risked his neck to get out of prison. He must've met those two *hombres*. Before he died, he told them things. And it's my idea, Sleeper, that what that chart tells is the location of the cache where Mendoza put away the whole savin's of his life."

The teeth of Lowry clicked together. His eyes grew green with bright greed. "Mendoza never spent nothin'. He never did nothin' but save," he added. "Sleeper, I've got three of my best men, and they're gonna ride with you, when you start the game."

"I work a lone hand or I don't work at all," said Sleeper dreamily, as he lay stretched on his bed, peering steadily out the window.

"Damn it," growled Lowry, "if you try to handle the two of 'em, they'll sure bust you full of lead. Mendoza never had nothin' to do with gents that wasn't murderers. Those are two gunmen, Sleeper, and, when you handled 'em before, you was dealin' with rattlers without knowin' it."

"I'll handle 'em alone or not at all," said Sleeper in the same voice.

"Sleeper. . . you'll carry a gun, then, won't you?"

Sleeper shook his head. "Any fool can carry a gun," he answered. "The fun of the game is handling fire with your bare hands."

There was a muffled, snarling sound from Pop Lowry. Then he strode from the room without another word.

Five minutes later Sleeper shuddered. For a man with a long, linen duster on had just stepped through the front door of the post office. The duster covered him very efficiently, but a certain weight about the shoulders, a certain sense of power in the arms was not lost on

155

Sleeper.

He was off his bed, down the stairs, and instantly in the stable behind the hotel. A moment later he had jerked the saddle on the back of the stallion and snapped the bridle over his head. Then he hurried down the alley and crossed into the vacant lot beside the hotel where a clump of tall shrubs covered him. He could see without being seen. He had hardly taken his post before the man in the linen duster came out from the post office again, paused to yawn widely, glanced up and down the street with quick eyes, and turned the corner.

Sleeper, running to the same corner, had a glimpse of two men swinging on the backs of two fine horses. At once the pair swung away at a rapid canter.

They left Weldon, headed north for five miles, swung sharply to the west, then went straight south through the mountains. For two days, Sleeper shivered in the wet winds and the whipping rains of the high ravines, following his quarry.

It was close work, dangerous work. Sometimes in a naked valley he had to let the pair get clear out of sight before he ventured to take the trail again. Once, coming through a dense fog which was simply a cloud entangled in the heights, he came suddenly around a rock face to face with a starry light. Through the mist, not five steps away, he heard the loud voice of Buzz Mahoney yell out: "Who's there? What's that?"

"A mountain sheep, you fool," suggested Tim Riley.

Ⓥ Ⓥ Ⓥ Ⓥ Ⓥ

Six days out of Weldon, Sleeper was riding anxiously through a ravine that was cluttered with such a litter of rocks that danger might have hidden there in the form of

156

whole regiments. It was only the hair-trigger sensitiveness of the nose of the stallion that detected trouble ahead. He stopped, jerked up his head, and the next instant Sleeper saw the wavering of sunlight on a bit of steel, the blue brightness of a leveled gun.

He whirled Careless away. Two rifles barked, sent long, clanging echoes down the ravine, and Sleeper swayed slowly out from the saddle, dropped, and hung head down with trailing arms, his right leg hooked over the saddle as though caught in the stirrup leather and so precariously was supported.

The rifles spoke no more. Instead, two riders began to clatter furiously in pursuit. A good mile they rushed their swift horses along, but Careless, with his master still hanging at his side, widened the distance of his lead with every strike, and finally was lost to view among the sea of boulders.

After that, the noise of the pursuit no longer beat through the ravine. Sleeper pulled himself back into the saddle. His leg ached as though the bone had been broken; his head spun; but there was no real harm done by his maneuver. He turned again on the trail. All that Pop Lowry had told him, all that he could have guessed, was reinforced doubly now. For when men would not delay to capture such a horse as Careless when the rider was apparently wounded to death, it was sure proof that Mahoney and Riley were bound toward a great goal.

Ⓥ Ⓥ Ⓥ Ⓥ Ⓥ

They went on securely, now, but steadily. They cleaved through the mountains, following the high Lister Pass, and then they dipped down along the side of the range into the terrible sun mist and dusty glare of

157

Alkali Flat.

Imagine a bowl a hundred miles across, rimmed with cool blue distance on either side, but paved with white heat and the welter and dance of the reflected sun. That was Alkali Flat.

Sleeper, looking from the rim of the terrible depression, groaned softly. He glanced up and saw three soaring buzzards come over the head of the mountain, turn, and sweep with untroubled wings back the way they had come. Even at that height, they seemed to dread the pungent heat that poured up from the vast hollow.

Sleeper, sitting in the shadow of a rock, sat down to think. He could find no resource in his mind. There was no way in which he could travel out into the desert. Whoever had chosen to hide a treasure in the midst of such an ocean of despair had chosen well. In the middle of the day, a man needed three pints of water an hour. A fellow whose canteen went dry in the middle of that hell would be mad with thirst by the time he had walked fifteen miles, at the most.

They went mad and died—every man the same way. The first act was to tear off the shirt. The second was to commence digging with bare hands in the sand and the rocks. They would be found that way afterward, the nails broken from their fingers, the flesh tattered, the very bones at the tips of the fingers splintered by the frightful, blind efforts of the dying men.

Sleeper, remembering one dreadful picture he had seen, slowly ran the pink tip of his tongue across his lips and sat up to breathe more easily. He had a canteen that would hold a single quart—and the valley was a hundred miles across! He had saddlebags, of course. They were new and strong, of the heaviest canvas. He took a pair of them and went to the nearest sound of running water. He drank and drank again of that delightfully bubbling spring; the mere sight of Alkali Flat had implanted in him an insatiable thirst. Then he filled one of the bags. The canvas was perfectly water-tight, but the seams let the water spurt out in streams.

He looked about him, not in despair, but with the sense of one condemned. If he could not enter the desert assured of a fair chance of getting through, why, he would enter it without that chance and trust to luck like a madman. He was drawn by that perverse hunger for danger like a dizzy man by the terrible edge of a cliff.

Then he saw the pine trees which were filling the mountain air with sweetness, and he remembered their resin. Resin? It exuded from them in little fresh runs; it dripped from the wounded bark; it flavored the air with its clean scent. He began to collect it rapidly with his knife, and, as he got it, he commenced to smear the stuff over the seams of his saddlebags, which he turned inside out. He had two pairs, and he resined all four in hardly more than an hour. That was why the stallion was well weighted down with a load of the purest spring water, going down the slope toward Alkali Flat.

His master went ahead of him, jauntily, whistling a little, but the heat from the desert already was beginning to sting the eyes and make the lids of them tender.

## VI
### "THE TREASURE"

IN ALKALI FLAT, THE EARTH WAS NOT A MOTHER. IT was a grave. Once there had been a river running through it; now there was only the hollow trough filled with the dead bones of the stream. Once there had been trees; now there were only the scarecrow trunks of a few ancient survivors. It was worse than the Sahara, because in the Sahara there was never life and here there was a ghost of it.

As Sleeper passed down into the frightful glare of that wasted land, he saw the trail of Mahoney and Tim Riley lead up to the bank of the dead river and then pass down the length of it. He felt that he knew, at once, the nature of the windings which had been depicted on the chart, and he could not help admiring the cleverness of Joe Mendoza, leaving his treasure here in the middle of a salt waste.

The temperature was above a hundred. That is a phrase which people use casually, liberally, without understanding. Actually, every part of a degree above blood heat begins to draw the strength from the heart. A dry heat is then an advantage in a sense, because the quick evaporation of the perspiration cools the flesh a little.

The heat in the great Alkali Flat was above a hundred and twenty. There were twenty-two degrees of fatal heat, and the dryness not merely turned sweat into mist at once, it laid hold on the flesh like a thousand leeches, sucking out the liquid from the body.

The feet of Sleeper began to burn in his boots. There seemed to be sand under his eyelids. The drying lips threatened to crack wide open. Thirst blew down his throat like a dusty wind at every breath he drew. At the same time, the skin of his face commenced to pull and contract, and the dry skin of his body was rubbed and chafed by his clothes.

Careless, indomitable in all conditions, now held on his way with his ears laid flat against his skull.

When Sleeper looked up, he saw a wedge of three

buzzards sliding out from the mountain height and hanging in the air. They might shun the air above the horrible flat, but not when foolish living creatures attempted to cross the floor of the oven. What insane beings, even a Mahoney and a Riley, ventured on such a journey by the light of the day?

Sleeper looked from the dizzy sky back to the earth. It was like a kitchen yard, a yard on which thousands of gallons of soapy water, in the course of generations, have been flung upon a summer-baked soil thrice a day. For a singular odor rose from the ground. And it was everywhere gray-white.

Along the banks of the river one could see where water had once flowed at varying levels. The banks had been eaten back by the now dead stream. Here and there, at the edges of the levels, appeared the dry roots of long-vanished plants and trees, as fine as hair.

There was no steady breeze, but now and again a twist of the air sucked up dust in a small air pool that moved with swiftness for a short distance and then melted away. If one of those white phantoms swayed toward Sleeper, he swerved the horse to avoid it. Careless himself shrank from the contact, for the alkali dust burned the passages of nose and lungs and mouth like dry lye, and the eyes were eaten by that unslaked lime.

Yet the other pair still advanced more deeply into that fire. An hour went by, and another, and another, and another. At a walk or a dog-trot, Careless stuck to his work. His coat was beginning to stare as his sweat dried and the salt of the perspiration stiffened the gloss of his hair. When Sleeper stroked the glorious neck of the horse, a thin dust followed his hand.

They had passed the danger point, long ago. That is to

161

say, they had passed the point when a man could safely attempt to journey out of the alkali hell without water to carry. A fellow with a two-quart canteen, no matter how he nursed it, would probably be frantic for liquid before he reached the promise of the mountains which, already, were turning brown and blue in the distance.

And then the two figures far ahead, only discernible in the spyglass which Sleeper now and then used for spotting them, dipped away from the flat and disappeared. They had descended into the stream bed. It might mean that they had spotted the pursuer and were going to stalk him in ambush. It might mean, also, that they had reached the proper bend of the dry draw and that they were about to search for the marked spot on the chart.

Sleeper, taking a chance on the second possibility, pushed Careless ahead rapidly until he was close to the point of the disappearance. Conscience, duty, a strange spirit seemed to ride in his shadow and drive him ahead, but his conscious mind rebelled against this torment. It told him to rush away toward one of those spots of cool, blue mirage that continually wavered into view on the face of the desert; it told him that all was useless, wealth, fame, honor no more real than the welter of the heat waves. But he kept on.

When he was reasonably close, he dipped Careless down into the channel of the vanished river, and watered him from the second saddlebag. The water was now almost the heat of blood, and it had developed a foul taste from cooking inside the heavy canvas, but Careless supped up the water greedily until the bag was empty. There remained to Sleeper one half of his original supply, and yet one half of his labor had not been completed.

162

Under a steep of the bank where there was a fall of shadow, he placed the horse and made him lie down. But the shadow was not a great blessing. The dimness seemed to thicken the air; it was like breathing dust, and the sand, even under the shadow, was hot to the touch. Here Careless was left, lifting his head and sending after his master a whinny of anxiety, no louder than a whisper. For the stallion knew as well as any man the reason those buzzards wheeled in the stillness of the hot air above.

Would the two men ahead take heed of the second group of buzzards? Or would they fail to notice, earthbound as their eyes must be, that the vultures wheeled and sailed in two parts?

Sleeper went on swiftly, but with care. And he could wish, now, that he had not left Weldon with empty hands. He had his knife, to be sure, and if he came to close range, that heavy knife with its needle-sharp point would be as deadly in his hands as any gun. It might well dispose of one of the pair, but the second one would certainly take revenge for his fall.

Very clearly, Sleeper knew what it meant if the couple were real companions of Joe Mendoza, that super-murderer. He would have none about him except savages as brutal as wild beasts. He would have none except experts in slaughter.

This knowledge made the step of Sleeper lighter than the step of a wildcat as he heard, directly around the next bend, the sound of blows sinking into the earth. From the sharp edge of the bank he saw, as he peered around it, both Mahoney and tall Tim Riley hard at work with a pick and a shovel which they had taken from their packs.

Their two horses, like the stallion, had been placed

163

under the partial shadow of the western bank. One stood head down, like a dying thing; the other, with more of the invincible Western toughness supporting its knees and its spirit, wandered with slow steps down the draw, sniffing curiously at the strange dead roots that projected here and there from the bank.

The two workers, hard at it, had now opened a good-size hole in the earth, and they were driving it deeper and deeper when Mahoney uttered a wild cry and flung both arms above his head. Then, leaning, he tore at something buried in the earth. There was the brittle noise of the rending of a tough fabric; Mahoney jerked up, holding what seemed a torn strip of tarpaulin in his hands, and leaned immediately to grasp it again. Riley helped him. They were both yelling out senseless, meaningless words.

Now Sleeper saw a very strange thing to do, and did it. He slipped quietly out from his post of vantage and went up to the horse which was wandering with slow steps down the bank, the water sloshing with soft gurglings inside the burlap-wrapped huge canteen that hung from the saddle.

Sleeper took the horse calmly by the bridle and led it, step by step, around the bend. He had the horse almost out of view, when Mahoney, leaping to his feet, apparently looked straight at the thief.

Instead of drawing a gun, Buzz Mahoney pulled off his hat and began to wave it and shout with delight. Tim Riley also commenced to prance around like a crazy man.

"The whole insides of the Levison Bank!" yelled Riley. "Kid, we got it! We're rich for life!"

They were blind with happiness. That was why Mahoney had failed to see the thief in his act of stealing, and now Sleeper was walking steadily down the draw with the horse behind him. He kept on until he reached the great stallion, which rose eagerly to meet him and touched noses with the other horse. Then Sleeper mounted Careless and put two miles of steady cantering behind him. After that, he rode up the bank to the level of the ground above and waited.

He sat in the shade under the side of Careless and ventured to smoke a cigarette that filled his lungs with a milder fire than that of the alkali dust.

One horse, two men, and the long, burning stretch of the desert to cross before the blue peace of the mountains surrounded them. It seemed to Sleeper that there was nothing in the world so beautiful as mountains, these mountains to the north. Yes, perhaps there were other regions even more delightful. There were the great Arctic and Antarctic plains where the ice of ages is piled. But to lie all day where water can flow across the body, where the lips can draw up clear water every moment—that is a bliss beyond words. It was easy to think, also, of the cool shadowy interiors of saloons, and the refreshing pungency of beer. Barrels of beer buried in vast casks of chipped ice and snow.

Men of sense should work with ice. What happy fellows are those who deliver the great, white, ponderous cakes of it, sawing and splitting it up for customers, drifting comfortably from house to house.

Ⓥ Ⓥ Ⓥ Ⓥ Ⓥ

Time passed. He watered the two horses and himself drank sparingly. There was still plenty of sun. It was high, high above the horizon, and those two fellows who had found the treasure of Joe Mendoza did not seem, as yet, to have discovered the loss of the second horse with more than half of their remaining water supply. Well, the wind of joy would cool them for a spell, but afterward. . . .

He thought, too, of the old, white-headed banker, level-eyed, fearless of the hatred that men poured on him since the failure of his bank after the robbery. What fools the officers of the law had been not to suspect that the job was that of Mendoza. Three men shot down wantonly. That was like Mendoza—Riley and Mahoney were no doubt of the murderous crew that attended the chief on that day of the hold-up.

It all made a simple picture, now. Escaping with their spoil, Mendoza had attended to the hiding of it. They would disappear from the face of the land for a time. Then, at an appointed date, they would gather. But, in the meantime, Mendoza had been captured on some other charge. He had been put into the prison, and, when he attempted to break out at the allotted moment, he had been shot. He had passed on his information, loyally, to his two men.

That was the story, and Sleeper knew it as well as though he had heard it from the lips of the pair.

And now, at last, the two came up over the edge of the draw and started toward the mountains, one of them in the saddle, the other riding behind.

Sleeper fell in with them.

That terrible dryness of the air, that flaming of the sun no longer seemed hostile. It was performing his work. At the end of a long, long hour, the mountains seemed even farther away than they had been at the beginning. Sleeper saw the pair halt. They took off the big canteen from the side of their horse, drank, and then appeared to be measuring out some of the liquid for the horse.

From half a mile away, Sleeper distinctly could see the flash of the priceless water as it was poured. He could see the poor horse shake its head with eagerness for more. Then tall Tim Riley fastened the canteen back in its place beside the saddle. This was the moment that Buzz Mahoney, snatching out a holstered rifle from the other side of the saddle, dropped to his knee and began to pour shot after shot at Sleeper.

But Sleeper, at a thousand yards, laughed, and the laughter was a dry whisper in his throat. He took off his hat and waved it, as though in encouragement. And the two remounted, and went on.

## VII
## "BLAZING GUNS"

FOR NEARLY ANOTHER HOUR, SLEEPER TRAVELED IN the wake of the pair, and still they seemed to be laboring in vain, never bringing the mountains closer.

Then trouble struck suddenly. They had dismounted to take water and give it to the horse again, when Sleeper saw by their gestures that they were in a heated argument. Two guns flashed like two dancing bits of blue flame. Then he saw Mahoney fall on his face; afterward the swift rattle of the reports struck his ear.

Tim Riley mounted and continued on his way, looking back toward the spot where his victim lay.

Sleeper, for some reason, looked suddenly up toward the buzzards that wheeled softly in the sky above him. They would be fed. But the figure of Mahoney now lifted from the ground. He ran a few steps in pursuit of Riley, and the small sound of his distant wailing came into the ears of Sleeper. To get mercy from Riley was an impossibility which not even the bewildered brain of a wounded man could entertain long. Sleeper, with a queer sickness of the heart, saw Mahoney tear the shirt from his back and fall to digging in the sand. Already the shock and the pain of bullet wounds, the swift loss of blood, and the burning caustic of Alkali Flat had reduced him to the madness of famine.

Sleeper came up rapidly, calling out. He was almost at the point where Mahoney groveled in the sand on his knees, scooping at the earth with his hands, before the wounded man looked up. He saw Sleeper with the bewilderment with which he might have stared at a heavenly angel. Then he came with a scream of hope, distending his mouth and eyes, his arms thrown out.

Blood ran down his body, which was swollen with strength rather than with fat. But he disregarded his wounds until he had drunk deeply. Then, recovering his wits a little, he looked rather vaguely up to Sleeper.

"You're still back on the trail, eh?" said Mahoney. "Leave me ride that other horse, will you?"

"You can ride it, if you want," agreed Sleeper.

There might have been twenty murders on the hands of this fellow, but still Sleeper pitied him.

Mahoney grasped the pommel of the saddle on the led horse, but suddenly weakness overcame him. He looked down with a singular wonder at the blood that rolled down his body. Those wounds were beyond curing, as Sleeper had seen at a glance. Mahoney realized it now, also, and the realization struck him down to his knees. He slumped to the side, his mouth open as he dragged at the hot, dusty air.

Sleeper, dismounting, knelt by him.

Mahoney cursed him. "Leave me be. I'm cooked," he said. "Go get Riley. Riley. . . he murdered me. I'm the eleventh man on his list. Him and Mendoza was like a

168

coupla brothers. If I could live to see Riley crawl. . . . I sure surprised him with my second shot. He's hurt. And them that are hurt in Alkali Flat. . . ."

He dropped flat on his back, and Sleeper thought that he was gone. But after a moment he spoke again, saying: "He thinks he'll get loose. . . but in Alkali Flat . . . death. . . death. . . will get through a scratch on the skin. Riley. . . Riley. . . ." A little shudder went through him as though he had been touched by cold.

And Sleeper turned to remount, for he knew that Mahoney was dead.

Ⓥ Ⓥ Ⓥ Ⓥ Ⓥ

Had Buzz really struck Tim Riley with one of his bullets? It seemed very likely, considering that they had exchanged shots almost hand to hand. Yet Tim Riley was voyaging steadily on across the Flat.

The mountains were closer, now. They had lost their blueness entirely and turned brown. Clouds covered the heads of some of the peaks—a paradise of happiness to wander, however blindly, through the cool dampness of a fog like that above! But in Alkali Flat the heat increased. The life was gone from the air, like the taste from overcooked food. But as the sun slanted from a deeper position in the west, a sort of mist seemed to cover the desert. That was the dust, made visible in the slanting sun rays just as the motes grow visible in the sun shaft that strikes through a window in winter. And this film of dust was what made breathing so difficult, perhaps.

Mahoney was dead. A division of the buzzards had dropped toward the ground, but still others trailed after Tim Riley. Had they scented the death that might even

169

now be working in the body of Riley?

As Mahoney had well said, through the smallest scratch death could enter the bodies of men in Alkali Flat. Where the struggle for mere existence was so hard, the slightest wound, the slightest extra drain on the strength might prove fatal.

Yet Tim Riley, so far as Sleeper could see, even through the glass, rode erect and steady.

Sleeper closed his thousand yards of safety to a quarter of a mile to study the gunman. He had a strong feeling that he was about to lose his long battle. For now the mountains rose like a wall against the sky; the heat of the sun was diminishing; twilight would unroll like a blessing across Alkali Flat before long, and Tim Riley would be among the slopes of the foothills, hunting for the sound of running water in the night, climbing steadily toward a purer, cooler air.

Where the flat ended, Sleeper saw the white streak of it just ahead, like a watermark drawn across the hills. Tim Riley was approaching that mark when, all at once, Sleeper saw that the horse was plodding on with downward head, as before, but with an empty saddle. But no, it was not empty. The rider had slumped well forward and lay out on the neck of the horse. It might be a bit of playing 'possum, Sleeper thought. For Riley must have realized that his pursuer was not armed, and now this might be a device to draw the other into easy range.

So Sleeper pressed forward only slowly until he noticed that the buzzards were swaying lower and lower through the air above the head of the fugitive. As though they conveyed a direct message to him, Sleeper lost all fear at once and closed in abruptly.

As he came, he saw the rider slipping slowly, inch by

170

inch, toward the side. When Sleeper came up, he waited until he actually had a hand on the shoulder of Tim Riley before he called out. But Tim Riley continued to lie prone, as though resting from a great fatigue.

He was resting, indeed, for he was dead.

When Sleeper stopped the horses at the base of the first foothill, he found that Tim Riley had been shot deeply through the body, a wound that might not have been fatal under ordinary circumstances, but which surely meant death in Alkali Flat. Riley had known that. He had lashed himself in his saddle. With his hands on the pommel, he had ridden erect, keeping his face toward safety and the mountains.

The mere instinct to keep on fighting had driven him on. A queer admiration crept through the heart of Sleeper as he looked at the lean, hard face of Riley, still set and grim and purposeful in death, with a long-distance look in his eyes, as though he were sighting some goal on the great journey on which he was now embarked.

In the saddlebag strapped behind the saddle was what Sleeper had struggled and striven so hard to reach. He knew that but left the thing untouched, while he urged the tired horse up the hill. He walked beside the horse that carried the dead man, to make sure that the body did not slip to the ground. A last, grim hour they struggled up that slope until Sleeper heard the sound of running water. A moment later the horses were standing belly-deep in a pool of blue, while Sleeper drank and drank again from the rivulet that fed the little lake.

By the side of that lake he buried Tim Riley by the simple device of laying the body under a boulder above which a little slide of rocks was hanging. A few stones moved, and that slide was launched. Fifty tons of débris rushed down over the spot where Riley lay, and his funeral oration was the flying echoes which talked and sang busily together for a few seconds all along the cañon.

Ⓥ Ⓥ Ⓥ Ⓥ Ⓥ

By the little pool, when it was holding the stars and the thin yellow flickering of the campfire, Sleeper ate hard tack, drank coffee, and examined the contents of the big saddlebag.

It was, in fact, the savings of an entire life of crime. He counted, bill by bill, three hundred and fifteen thousand dollars of hard cash. In addition, there were a number of jewels, choice stones, which had been broken out of their settings.

The blood began to beat fast in the temples of Sleeper.

## VIII
## "FUN FOR SLEEPER"

LEVISON, PRESIDENT AND CHIEF SHAREHOLDER IN the Levison Bank of Tucker Flat, still went down to his office every day. He carried himself exactly as he had done when the lifting of his finger was enough to control the wild men and the strong men of Tucker Flat. He had a short, black mustache, his eyebrows and eyes were black, but his hair was a thin cloud of white. He was a narrow, tall, straight man who had looked the world in the face for so many years that disaster could not teach him to bow his head. When he walked down the street now, people scowled at him, they cursed him in audible undertones, but he walked neither more

172

quickly nor more slowly. His wife knew that Levison was dying of a broken heart, but he was dying on his feet.

Every day he went down to the bank, unlocked the front door, walked past the grille work of gilded steel, past the empty cages of the cashier and clerk, and into his own office, where he unlocked his desk and waited.

Sometimes he was there all day, and nothing happened. Often someone entered to talk over the recent robbery and to curse Levison for not guarding the treasures of others more securely. Levison used to answer: "If there is any fault, it is mine. You have a right to denounce me. No man should dare to fail in this world of ours." He kept his chin high, while grief like an inward wolf devoured his heart.

On this day, his walk down the street had been particularly a trial. For the unemployed from the closed mines were thick in the street, and they had learned to attribute their lack of a job to the failure of the bank which had shut up the mines. So they thronged thickly about Levison, shook their fists in his face, cursed him and all his ancestors. He went through them like a sleepwalker and never answered a word. Perhaps he hoped that one of the drunkards would strike him down and that the rest would pluck the life out of his body; it was not rooted very deep in his flesh, these days.

So, when he came to his office, he sat with his head bowed a little and his hands folded together on the edge of his desk. He wanted to die quickly, but there was that hollow-cheeked woman who waited for him in the house on the hill from which the servants had been discharged. Wherever she went, even into death, she would follow him not more than a step behind.

He heard the front door of the bank open in the

middle of the morning. A step sounded in the emptiness of the big outer room, and then a hand tapped at his door.

"Come in!" called Levison.

The door was pushed open by a slender young fellow with black hair and blue eyes. He was very brown of skin, erect of carriage, and his clothes were mere ragged patches. Over his shoulder he carried a saddlebag.

"Were you a depositor in my bank?" asked Levison, opening the usual formula.

"I never was, but I intend to be," said the stranger.

Levison frowned. "The bank has failed," he said gravely.

"Then we'd better bring it back to life again," said the other.

"Who are you?" snapped Levison.

"Name of Sleeper. And here's the stuff that Joe Mendoza and Tim Riley and Buzz Mahoney stole from your vault. All of that and a little more. How much did you lose?"

Levison rose slowly from his chair. He stared into the blue eyes of this young man, and it seemed to him that they were the blue of flame before it turns yellow.

"Two hundred and fifty-two thousand five hundred and fourteen dollars," he said. That number was written across his soul as across a parchment.

"Count it out of this lot, then," said Sleeper. "There's plenty more. And then tell me where the rest of the cash ought to go. . . or have I claim to it? It's the life savings of Mister Murderer Mendoza!"

Ⓥ Ⓥ Ⓥ Ⓥ Ⓥ

At the little shack outside the town of Tucker Flat, big

174

Pop Lowry strode back and forth and up and down. Three men waited near the small campfire, never speaking, looking curiously across at Lowry now and then.

"I been double-crossed," said Pop Lowry. "I ought to send you out on his trail right now. But I'm gonna wait to see has he got the nerve to come here and face me. I'm gonna wait another half hour."

"Hark at them sing!" said one of the men, lifting his head.

For from the town of Tucker Flat there poured distant rumblings and even thin, high-pitched, half-hysterical laughter.

For the bank of Levison had reopened, and the mines that had recovered their deposits were reopening, also. That was reason enough to make the men of Tucker Flat rejoice.

Here there was a slight noise of rustling leaves among the shrubbery, and then into the dimness of the firelight rode a man on a great golden stallion.

"Sleeper!" exclaimed Pop Lowry.

"Get the three of them out of the way," said Sleeper, halting Careless.

"Back up, boys," said the peddler. "Wait somewheres. . . somewheres that I can whistle to you."

The three rose, stared an instant at Sleeper like dogs marking a quarry, and then stalked away.

Sleeper went to the fire, rinsed a tin cup, and filled it with coffee. He made and lighted a cigarette to accompany the coffee, and blew the smoke into the air after a deep inhalation.

"Well?" said Lowry, growling. "You done yourself fine, I hear?"

"Who told you I did?" asked Sleeper.

175

"Nobody else would have got the money back. Nobody else would have got it back for Levison and then told him to swear not to use the name. *You* got the money Mendoza stole!"

"Levison has his quarter of a million," said Sleeper. "And there was something left over. You get half." He took out a sheaf of bills tied about by a piece of string and threw it like a stick of wood to the peddler.

"There's a shade over sixty thousand in that," said Sleeper. "Count out your half. Besides, there's this stuff. Levison says that I have a right to it. So you take half of this, too. . . seeing that I'm your hired man." He threw a little chamois sack into the hands of Lowry, who lifted his head once, and thrust out his long jaw before he began to reckon the treasure.

After that, he was employed for a long time. At last he looked up and said hoarsely: "Where's Mahoney?"

"In Alkali Flat," said Sleeper.

"Dead?"

"Yes."

"Where's Tim Riley?"

"In the hills near Alkali Flat."

"Dead?"

"Yes."

"You let 'em find the stuff, and then you took it away from 'em?"

"Yes."

"And you didn't use a gun?"

"No."

"What *did* you use?"

"The sun and the buzzards," said Sleeper.

Lowry rubbed a hand back across the bald spot of his head.

"You had the brains to do that. . . and you was still

176

fool enough to turn back a quarter of a million to that Levison?"

Sleeper sipped black coffee.

"You don't even get any glory out of it!" shouted Lowry. "You won't let Levison tell who done the job for him. There ain't a soul in the world but me that knows what you done!"

"Pop," said Sleeper, "glory is a dangerous thing for a fellow like me."

The peddler stared at him. "A hundred and twenty-five thousand to you. . . the same to me. . . and you throwed it away! You ain't human! You're a fool!"

Sleeper sipped more coffee and drew on his cigarette.

"Tell me," growled Pop Lowry. "What you expect to get out of life? If you don't want money, what *do* you want?"

"Fun," said Sleeper thoughtfully.

"This here hell trail, this here work you done in Alkali Flat that even the birds. . . save the buzzards. . . won't fly over. . . was that fun? Where was the fun in that?"

"The look in the eyes of Levison," said Sleeper thoughtfully. "That was the fun for me, Pop."

# BLONDY

*As a popular storyteller, Faust began selling to the Munsey pulp magazines in 1917. By 1920 he'd branched out to Street & Smith, but none of his stories had appeared in the higher-paying, slick-paper market. His first sale to the slicks was a novel, "Alcatraz," which was placed in* **Country Gentleman** *in 1922. Then it was back to the pulps—until early 1924 when Faust achieved his second slick-paper sale to* **Collier's**, *one of the nation's top magazines. "Blondy" was originally printed as "Bulldog" in the February 23, 1924 issue and featured a white bull terrier. It precedes "A Lucky Dog," by some three years. By the mid-1930s Faust was selling steadily to all of the major slick markets, but such placements were unusual in the 1920s. Reading "Blondy" today, one can see why* **Collier's** *purchased this story. Its protagonist, Peter Zinn, is a cold, harsh, cruel man, who values strength above all else, with no room in his life for love or sentiment. Then a white bull terrier named Blondy, with a fighting spirit equal to Zinn's own, enters the big man's life and forces him to confront a new reality. The thundering climax is Faust at his fast-action best—as man and beast achieve their full potential. Once read, never forgotten. Here is yet another vigorous, powerfully-realized tale from the hand of a master storyteller.*

WHEN ZINN CAME HOME FROM PRISON, NO ONE WAS at the station to meet him except the constable, Tom Frejus, who laid a hand on his shoulder and said: "Now,

Zinn, let this here be a lesson to you. Give me a chance to treat you white. I ain't going to hound you. Just remember that because you're stronger than other folks you ain't got any reason to beat them up."

Zinn looked down upon him from a height. Every day of the year during which he swung his sledge-hammer to break rocks for the state roads, he had told himself that one good purpose was served: his muscles grew harder, the fat dropped from his waist and shoulders, the iron square of his chin thrust out as in his youth, and, when he came back to town, he would use that strength to wreak upon the constable his old hate. For manifestly Tom Frejus was his arch-enemy. When he first came to Sioux Crossing and fought the three men in Joe Riley's saloon—oh, famous and happy night!—Constable Frejus gave him a warning. When he fought the Gandil brothers and beat them both senseless, Frejus arrested him. When his old horse, Fidgety, balked in the back lot and Zinn tore a rail from the fence in lieu of a club, Tom Frejus arrested him for cruelty to dumb beasts. This was a crowning torment, for, as Zinn told the judge, he'd bought that old skate with good money and he had a right to do what he wanted with it. But the judge, as always, agreed with Tom Frejus. These incidents were only items in a long list which culminated when Zinn drank deep of bootleg whiskey and then beat up the constable himself. The constable, at the trial, pleaded for clemency on account, he said, of Zinn's wife and three children; but Zinn knew, of course, that Frejus wanted him back only that the old persecution might begin. On this day, therefore, the ex-convict, in pure excess of rage, smiled down on the constable.

"Keep out of my way, Frejus," he said, "and you'll keep a whole skin. But some day I'll get you alone, and

179

then I'll bust you in two. . . like this!"

He made an eloquent gesture, then he strode off up the street. As the sawmill had just closed, a crowd of returning workers swarmed on the sidewalks, and Zinn took off his cap so that they could see his cropped head. In his heart of hearts he hoped that some one would jibe, but the crowd split away before him and passed with cautiously averted eyes. Most of them were big, rough fellows, and their fear was pleasant balm for his savage heart. He went on with his hands a little tensed to feel the strength of his arms.

Ⓥ Ⓥ Ⓥ Ⓥ Ⓥ

The dusk was closing early on this autumn day with a chill whirl of snowflakes borne on a wind that had been iced in crossing the heads of the white mountains, but Zinn did not feel the cold. He looked up to the black ranks of the pine forest which climbed the sides of Sandoval Mountain, scattering toward the top and pausing where the sheeted masses of snow began. Life was like that—a struggle, an eternal fight, but never a victory on the mountaintop which all the world could see and admire. When the judge sentenced him, he said: "If you lived in the days of armor, you might have been a hero, Zinn. . . but in these times you are a waster and an enemy of society." He had grasped dimly at the meaning of this. Through his life he had always aimed at something which would set him apart from and above his fellows; now, at the age of forty, he felt in his hands an undiminished authority of might, but still those hands had not given him the victory. If he beat and routed four men in a huge conflict, society, instead of applauding, raised the club of the law and struck him down. It had

180

always done so, but, although the majority voted against him, his tigerish spirit groped after and clung to this truth: to be strong is to be glorious!

He reached the hilltop and looked down to his home in the hollow. A vague wonder and sorrow came upon him to find that all had been held together in spite of his absence. There was even a new coat of paint upon the woodshed, and a hedge of young firs was growing neatly around the front yard. In fact, the homestead seemed to be prospering as though his strength were not needed. He digested this reflection with an oath and looked sullenly about him. On the corner a little white dog watched him with lowered ears and a tail curved under its belly.

"Get out, cur!" snarled Zinn. He picked up a rock and threw it with such good aim that it missed the dog by a mere inch or two, but the puppy merely pricked its ears and straightened its tail.

"It's silly with the cold," said Zinn to himself, chuckling. "This time I'll smear it."

He pried from the roadway a stone of three or four pounds, took good aim, and hurled it as lightly as a pebble flies from the sling. Too late the white dog leaped to the side, for the flying missile caught it a glancing blow that tumbled it over and over. Zinn, muttering with pleasure, scooped up another stone, but, when he raised it this time, the stone fell from his hand, so great was his surprise. The white dog, with a line of red along its side where a ragged edge of the stone had torn the skin, had gained its feet and now was driving silently straight at the big man. Indeed, Zinn had barely time to aim a kick at the little brute, which it dodged as a rabbit turns from the jaw of the hound. Then two rows of small, sharp teeth pierced his trousers and sank into the flesh of his leg. He uttered a yell of surprise rather than pain. He kicked the swaying, tugging creature, but still it clung, working the puppy teeth deeper with intent devotion. He picked up a fallen stone and brought it down heavily with a blow that laid open the skull and brought a gush of blood, but, although the body of the little savage grew limp, the jaws were locked. He had to pry them apart with all his strength. Then he swung the loose, senseless body into the air by the hind legs.

What stopped him he could not tell. Most of all it was the stabbing pain in his leg and the marvel that so small a dog could have dared so much. But at last he tucked it under his arm, regardless of the blood that trickled over his coat. He went down the hill, kicked open the front door, and threw down his burden. Mrs. Zinn was coming from the kitchen with a shrill cry that sounded more like fear than like a welcome to Zinn.

"Peter! Peter!" she cried at him, clasping her hands together and staring.

"Shut up your yapping," said Peter Zinn. "Shut up and take care of this pup. He's my kind of a dog."

His three sons wedged into the doorway and gaped at him with round eyes and white faces.

"Look here," he said, pointing to his bleeding leg, "that damned pup done that. That's the way I want you kids to grow up. Fight anything. Fight a buzz saw. You don't need to go to no school for lessons. You can foller after Blondy, there."

So Blondy was christened; so he was given a home. Mrs. Zinn, who had been a trained nurse in her youth, nevertheless stood by with moans of sympathy while her husband took the necessary stitches in the head of Blondy.

"Keep still, fool," said Mr. Zinn. "Look at Blondy.

182

He ain't even whining. Pain don't hurt nothing. Pain is the making of a dog. . . or a man! Look at there. . . if he ain't licking my hand! He knows his master!"

Ⓥ Ⓥ Ⓥ Ⓥ Ⓥ

A horse kicked old Joe Harkness the next day, and Peter Zinn took charge of the blacksmith shop. He was greatly changed by his stay in the penitentiary, so that superficial observers in the town of Sioux Crossing declared that he had been reformed by punishment, inasmuch as he no longer blustered or hunted fights in the streets of the village. He attended to his work, and as everyone admitted that no farrier in the country could fit horseshoes better, or do a better job at welding, when Joe Harkness returned to his shop, he kept Zinn as a junior partner. Peter Zinn did not waste time or money on bootleg whiskey, but in spite of these and manifold virtues some of the very observant declared that there was more to be feared from the silent and settled ferocity of his manner than from the boisterous ways which had been his in other days. Constable Tom Frejus was among the latter. And it was noted that he practiced half an hour every day with his revolver in the back of his lot.

Blondy, in the meantime, stepped into maturity in a few swift months. On his fore and hindquarters the big ropy muscles thrust out. His neck grew thicker and more arched, and in his dark brown eyes there appeared a wistful look of eagerness which never left him saving when Peter Zinn was near. The rest of the family he tolerated, but did not love. It was in vain that Mrs. Zinn, eager to please a husband whose transformation had filled her with wonder and awe, lavished attentions

183

upon Blondy and fed him with dainties twice a day. It was in vain that the three boys petted and fondled and talked kindly to Blondy. He endured these demonstrations, but did not return them. When five o'clock came in the evening of the day, Blondy went out to the gate of the front yard and stood there like a white statue until a certain heavy step sounded on the wooden sidewalk up the hill. That noise changed Blondy into an ecstasy of impatience, and, when the big man came through the gate, Blondy raced and leaped about him with such a muffled whine of joy, coming from such depths of his heart, that his whole body trembled. At meals Blondy lay across the feet of the master. At night he curled into a warm circle at the foot of the bed.

Ⓥ Ⓥ Ⓥ Ⓥ Ⓥ

There was only one trouble with Blondy. When people asked—"What sort of dog is that?"—Peter Zinn could never answer anything except—"A hell of a good fighting dog. . . you can lay to that." It was a stranger who finally gave them information, a lumber merchant who had come to Sioux Crossing to buy timberland. He stopped Peter Zinn on the street and crouched on his heels to admire Blondy.

"A real white one," he said. "As fine a bull terrier as I ever saw. What does he weigh?"

""Fifty-five pounds," said Zinn.

"I'll give you five dollars for every pound of him," said the stranger.

Peter Zinn was silent.

"Love him too much to part with him, eh?" asked the other, smiling up at the big blacksmith.

"Love him?" snorted Zinn. "Love a dog! I ain't no fool."

"Ah?" said the stranger. "Then what's your price?"

Peter Zinn scratched his head, then he scowled, for when he tried to translate Blondy into terms of money, his wits failed him. "That's two hundred and seventy-five dollars," he said finally.

"I'll make it three hundred, even. And, mind you, my friend, this dog is useless for show purposes. You've let him fight too much, and he's covered with scars. No trimming can make that right ear presentable. However, he's a grand dog, and he'd be worth something in the stud."

Zinn hardly heard the last of this. He was considering that for three hundred dollars he could extend the blacksmith shop by one-half and get a full partnership with Harkness, or else he could buy that four-cylinder car which young Thompson wanted to sell. Yet even the showy grandeur of an automobile would hardly serve. He did not love Blondy. Love was an emotion which he scorned as beneath the dignity of a strong man. He had not married his wife because of love, but because he was tired of eating in restaurants and because other men had homes. The possession of an automobile would put the stamp upon his new prosperity, but could an automobile welcome him home at night or sleep at his feet?

"I dunno," he said at last. "I guess I ain't selling."

And he walked on. He did not feel more kindly toward Blondy after this. In fact, he never mentioned the circumstance, even in his home, but often, when he felt the warmth of Blondy at his feet, he was both baffled and relieved.

In the meantime, Blondy had been making history in

Sioux Crossing hardly less spectacular than that of Zinn. His idea of play was a battle; his conception of a perfect day embraced the killing of two or three dogs. Had he belonged to anyone other than Zinn, he would have been shot before his career was well started, but his owner was such a known man that guns were handled but not used when the white terror came near. It could be said in his behalf that he was not aggressive and, unless urged on, would not attack another. However, he was a most hearty and capable finisher of a fight if one were started.

He first took the eye of the town through a fracas with Bill Curry's brindled bulldog, Mixer. Blondy was seven or eight pounds short of his magnificent maturity when he encountered Mixer and touched noses with him; the bulldog reached for Blondy's foreleg, snapped his teeth in the empty air, and the fun began. As Harkness afterward put it: "Mixer was like thunder, but Blondy was lightning on wheels." Blondy drifted around the heavier dog for five minutes as illusive as a phantom. Then he slid in, closed the long, pointed, fighting jaw on Mixer's gullet, and was only pried loose from a dead dog.

After that the great Dane that had been brought to town by Mr. Henry Justice, the mill owner, took the liberty of snarling at the white dog and had his throat torn out in consequence. When Mr. Justice applied to the law for redress, the judge told him frankly that he had seen the fight and that he would sooner hang a man than hang Blondy. The rest of the town was of the same opinion. They feared but respected the white slayer, and it was pointed out that although he battled like a champion against odds, yet when little Harry Garcia took Blondy by the tail and tried to tie a knot in it, the

186

great terrier merely pushed the little boy away with his forepaws and then went on his way.

$$\text{Ⓥ Ⓥ Ⓥ Ⓥ Ⓥ}$$

However, there was trouble in the air, and Charlie Kitchen brought it to a head. In his excursions to the north he had chanced upon a pack of hounds used indiscriminately to hunt and kill anything that walked on four legs, from wolves to mountain lions and grizzly bears. The leader of that pack was a hundred-and-fifty-pound monster—a cross between a gigantic timber wolf and a wolfhound. Charlie could not borrow that dog, but the owner himself made the trip to Sioux Crossing and brought Gray King, as the dog was called, along with him. Up to that time Sioux Crossing felt that the dog would never be born that could live fifteen minutes against Blondy, but, when the northerner arrived with a large roll of money and his dog, the town looked at Gray King and pushed its money deeper into its pocket. For the King looked like a fighting demon, and, in fact, was one. Only Peter Zinn had the courage to bring out a hundred dollars and stake it on the result.

They met in the vacant lot next to the post office where the fence was loaded with spectators, and in this ample arena it was admitted that the wolf dog would have plenty of room to display all of his agility. As a matter of fact, it was expected that he would slash the heart out of Blondy in ten seconds. Slash Blondy he did, for there is nothing canine in the world that can escape the lightning flash of a wolf's side rip. A wolf fights by charges and retreats, coming in to slash with its great teeth and try to knock down the foe with the blow of its shoulder. The Gray King cut Blondy twenty times, but

187

they were only glancing knife-edge strokes. They took the blood, but not the heart from Blondy, who, in the meantime, was placed too low and solidly on the ground to be knocked down. At the end of twenty minutes, as the Gray King leaped in, Blondy side-stepped like a dancing boxer, then dipped in and up after a fashion that Sioux Crossing knew of old, and set that low, punishing jaw in the throat of the King. The latter rolled, writhed, and gnashed the air, but fate had him by the windpipe, and in thirty seconds he was helpless. Then Peter Zinn, as a special favor, took Blondy off.

Afterward the big man from the north came to pay his bet, but Zinn, looking up from his task of dressing the terrier's wounds, flung the money back in the face of the stranger.

"Dogs ain't the only things that fight in Sioux Crossing," he announced, and the stranger, pocketing his pride and his money at the same time, led his staggering dog away.

From that time Blondy was one of the sights of the town—like Sandoval Mountain. He was pointed out constantly, and people said—"Good dog!"—from a distance, but only Tom Frejus appreciated the truth. He said: "What keeps Zinn from getting fight-hungry? Because he has a dog that does the fighting for him. Every time Blondy sinks his teeth in the hide of another dog, he helps to keep Zinn out of jail. But some day Zinn will bust through!"

This was hardly a fair thing for the constable to say, but the nerves of honest Tom Frejus were wearing thin. He knew that sooner or later the blacksmith would attempt to execute his threat of breaking him in two, and the suspense lay heavily upon Tom. He was still practicing steadily with his guns; he was still as confident as ever of his own courage and skill; but, when he passed on the street the gloomy face of the blacksmith, a chill of weakness entered his blood.

Ⓥ Ⓥ Ⓥ Ⓥ Ⓥ

That dread, perhaps, had sharpened the perceptions of Frejus, for certainly he had looked into the truth, and, while Peter Zinn bided his time, the career of Blondy was a fierce comfort to him. The choicest morsel of enjoyment was delivered into his hands on a morning in September, the very day after Frejus had gained lasting fame by capturing the two Minster brothers, with enough robberies and murders to their credit to have hanged a dozen men.

The Zinns took breakfast in the kitchen this Thursday, so that the warmth of the cook stove might fight the frost out of the air, and Oliver, the oldest boy, announced from the window that old Gripper, the constable's dog, had come into the back yard. The blacksmith rose to make sure. He saw Gripper, a big black-and-tan sheep dog, nosing the top of the garbage can, and a grin of infinite satisfaction came to the face of Peter Zinn. First, he cautioned the family to remain discreetly indoors. Then he stole out by the front way, came around to the rear of the tall fence that sealed his back yard, and closed and latched the gate. The trap was closed on Gripper, after which Zinn returned to the house and lifted Blondy to the kitchen window. The hair lifted along the back of Blondy's neck; a growl rumbled in the depths of his powerful body. Yonder was his domain, his own yard, of which he knew each inch—the smell of every weed and rock; yonder was the spot where he had killed the stray chicken last July; near it

189

was the tall, rank nettle, so terrible to an over-inquisitive nose; and, behold, a strange dog pawing at the very place where, only yesterday, he had buried a stout bone with a rich store of marrow hidden within.

"Oh, Peter, you ain't. . . ?" began Mrs. Zinn.

Her husband silenced her with an ugly glance, then he opened the back door and tossed Blondy into the yard. The bull terrier landed lightly and running. He turned into a white streak that crashed against Gripper, turned the latter head over heels, and tumbled the shepherd into a corner. Blondy wheeled to finish the good work, but Gripper lay at his feet, abject upon his belly, with ears lowered, head pressed between his paws, wagging a conciliatory tail and whining a confession of shame, fear, and humility. Blondy leaped at him with a stiff-legged jump and snapped his teeth at the very side of one of those drooped ears, but Gripper only melted a little closer to the ground. For, a scant ten days before, he had seen that formidable warrior, the Chippings's greyhound, throttled by the white destroyer. What chance would he have with his worn old teeth? He whined a sad petition through them, and, closing his eyes, he offered up a prayer to the god that watches over all good dogs: Never, never again would he rummage around a strange back yard, if only this one sin were forgiven.

The door of the house slammed open; a terrible voice was shouting: "Take him, Blondy! Kill him, Blondy!"

Blondy, with a moan of battle joy, rushed in again. His teeth clipped over the neck of Gripper, but the dreadful jaws did not close. For, even in this extremity, Gripper only whined and wagged his tail the harder. Blondy danced back.

"You damn quitter!" yelled Peter Zinn. "Tear him to

bits! Take him, Blondy!"

The tail of Blondy flipped from side to side to show that he had heard. He was shuddering with awful eagerness, but Gripper would not stir.

"Coward! Coward! Coward!" snarled Blondy. "Get up and fight. Here I am. . . half turned away. . . offering you the first hold. . . if you only dare to take it!"

Never was anything said more plainly in dog talk, saving the pitiful response of Gripper: "Here I lie. . . kill me if you will. I am an old, old man with worn-out teeth and a broken heart."

Blondy stopped snarling and trembling. He came a bit nearer, and with his own touched the cold nose of Gripper. The old dog opened one eye.

"Get up," said Blondy very plainly. "But if you dare to come near my buried bone again, I'll murder you, you old rip." And he lay down above that hidden treasure, wrinkling his eyes and lolling out his tongue, which, as all dogs know, is a sign that a little gambol and play will not be amiss.

"Dad!" cried Oliver Zinn. "He won't touch Gripper. Is he sick?"

"Come here!" thundered Zinn, and, when Blondy came, he kicked the dog across the kitchen and sent him crashing into the wall. "You yaller-hearted cur!" snarled Peter Zinn, and strode out of the house to go to work.

His fury did not abate until he had delivered a shower of blows with a fourteen-pound sledge upon a bar of cold iron on his anvil, wielding the ponderous hammer with one capacious hand. After that he was able to try to think it out. It was very mysterious. For his own part, when he was enraged, it mattered not what crossed his path—old and young, weak and strong, they were grist for the mill of his hands and he ground them small,

191

indeed. But Blondy, apparently, followed a different philosophy and would not harm those who were helpless.

Then Peter Zinn looked down to the foot that had kicked Blondy across the room. He was tremendously unhappy. Just why, he could not tell, but he fumbled at the mystery all that day and the next. Every time he faced Blondy, the terrier seemed to have forgotten that brutal attack, but Peter Zinn was stabbed to the heart by a brand new emotion—shame. And when he met Blondy at the gate on the second evening, something made him stoop and stroke the scarred head. It was the first caress. He looked up with a hasty pang of guilt and turned a dark red when he saw his wife watching from the window of the front bedroom. Yet, when he went to sleep that night, he felt that Blondy and he had been drawn closer together.

The very next day the crisis came. He was finishing his lunch, when guns began to bark and rattle—reports with a metallic and clanging overtone which meant that rifles were in play, then a distant shouting rolled confusedly upon them. Peter Zinn called Blondy to his heels and went out to investigate.

The first surmise that jumped into his mind had been correct. Jeff and Lew Minster had broken from jail, been headed off in their flight, and had taken refuge in the post office. There they held the crowd at bay, Jeff taking the front of the building and Lew the rear. Vacant lots surrounded the old frame shack since the general merchandise store burned down three years before, and the rifles of two expert shots commanded this no man's land. It would be night before they could close in on the building, but, when night came, the Minster boys would have an excellent chance of breaking away with darkness to cover them.

"What'll happen?" asked Tony Jeffreys of the blacksmith as they sat at the corner of the hotel where they could survey the whole scene.

"I dunno," said Peter Zinn, as he puffed at his pipe. "I guess it's up to the constable to show the town that he's a hero. There he is now!"

The constable had suddenly dashed out of the door of Sam Donoghue's house, directly facing the post office, followed by four others, in the hope that he might take the defenders by surprise. But when men defend their lives, they are more watchful than wolves in the hungry winter of the mountains. A Winchester spoke from a window of the post office the moment the forlorn hope appeared. The first bullet knocked the hat from the head of Harry Daniels and stopped him in his tracks. The second shot went wide. The third knocked the feet from under the constable and flattened him in the road. This was more than enough. The remnant of the party took to its heels and regained shelter safely before the dust raised by his fall had ceased curling above the prostrate body of the constable.

Tony Jeffreys had risen to his feet, repeating over and over an oath of his childhood—"Jiminy whiskers! Jiminy whiskers! They've killed poor Tom Frejus!"— but Peter Zinn, holding the tremblingly eager body of Blondy between his hands, jutted forth his head and grinned in a savage warmth of contentment.

"He's overdue," was all he said.

But Tom Frejus was not dead. His leg had been broken between the knee and hip, but he now reared himself upon both hands and looked about him. He had covered the greater part of the road in his charge. It would be easier to escape from fire by crawling close

193

under the shelter of the wall of the post office than by trying to get back to Donoghue's house. Accordingly, he began to drag himself forward. He had not covered a yard when the Winchester cracked again, and Tom crumpled on his face with both arms flung around his head.

Peter Zinn stood up with a gasp. Here was something quite different. The constable was beaten, broken, and he reminded Zinn of one thing only—old Gripper cowering against the fence with Blondy, towering above, ready to kill. Blondy had been merciful, but the heartless marksman behind the window was still intent on murder. His next bullet raised a white furrow of dust near Frejus. Then a wild voice, made thin and high by the extremity of fear and pain, cleft through the air and smote the heart of Peter Zinn: "Help! For God's sake, mercy!"

Tom Frejus was crushed, indeed, and begging as Gripper had begged. A hundred voices were shouting with horror, but no man dared venture out in the face of that cool-witted marksman. Then Peter Zinn knew the thing that he had been born to do, for which he had been granted strength of hand and courage of heart. He threw his long arms out before him as though he were running to embrace a bodiless thing; a great wordless voice swelled in his breast and tore his throat; and he raced out toward the fallen constable.

Some woman's voice was screaming: "Back! Go back, Peter! Oh, God, stop him! Stop him!"

Minster had already marked his coming. The rifle cracked, and a blow on the side of his head knocked Peter Zinn into utter blackness. A searing pain and the hot flow of blood down his face brought back his senses. He leaped to his feet again, heard a yelp of joy

194

as Blondy danced away before him, then he drove past the writhing body of Tom Frejus. The gun spoke again from the window; the red-hot torment stabbed him again, he knew not where. Then he reached the door of the building and gave his shoulder to it.

It was a thing of paper that ripped open before him. He plunged through into the room beyond, where he saw the long, snarling face of the younger Minster in the shadow of a corner with the gleam of the leveled rifle barrel. He dodged as the gun spat fire, heard a brief and wicked humming beside his ear, then scooped up in one hand a heavy chair, and flung it at the gunman.

Minster went down with his legs and arms sprawled in an odd position, and Peter Zinn gave him not so much as another glance for he knew that this part of his work was done.

"Lew! Lew!" cried a voice from the back of the building. "What's happened? What's up? D'you want help?"

"Aye!" shouted Peter Zinn. "He wants help. You damn' murderer, it's me. . . Peter Zinn! Peter Zinn!"

He kicked open the door beyond and ran full into the face of a lightning flash. It withered the strength from his body. He slumped down on the floor with his loose shoulders resting against the wall. In a twilight dimness he saw big Jeff Minster standing in a thin swirl of smoke with the rifle muzzle twitching down and steadying for the finishing shot, but a white streak leaped through the doorway, over his shoulder, and flew at Minster.

Before the sick eyes of Peter Zinn, the man and the dog whirled into a blur of darkness streaked with white. There passed two long, long seconds, thick with stampings, the wild curses of Jeff Minster, the deep and

195

humming growl of Blondy. Moreover, out of the distance a great wave of voices was rising, sweeping toward the building.

The eyes of Peter cleared. He saw Blondy fastened to the right leg of Jeff Minster above the knee. The rifle had fallen to the floor, and Jeff Minster, yelling with pain and rage, had caught out his hunting knife, had raised it. He stabbed. But still Blondy clung. "No, no!" screamed Peter Zinn.

"Your damned dog first. . . then you," gasped Minster.

The weakness struck Zinn again. His great head lolled back on his shoulders. "God," he moaned, "gimme strength! Don't let Blondy die!"

And strength poured hot upon his body, a strength so great that he could reach his hand to the rifle on the floor, gather it to him, put his finger on the trigger, and raise the muzzle, slowly, slowly, as though it weighed a ton.

The knife had fallen again. It was a half-crimson dog that still clung to the slayer. Feet beat, voices boomed like a waterfall in the next room. Then, as the knife rose again, Zinn pulled the trigger, blind to his target, and, as the thick darkness brushed across his brain, he saw something falling before him.

Ⓥ Ⓥ Ⓥ Ⓥ Ⓥ

He seemed, after a time, to be walking down an avenue of utter blackness. Then a thin star ray of light glistened before him. It widened. A door of radiance opened through which he stepped and found himself—lying between cool sheets with the binding grip of bandages holding him in many places and, wherever the bandages held, the deep, sickening ache of wounds. Dr. Burney leaned above him, squinting as though Peter Zinn were far away. Then Peter's big hand caught him.

"Doc," he said, "what's happened? Gimme the worst of it."

"If you lie quiet, my friend," said the doctor, "and husband your strength, and fight for yourself as bravely as you fought for Constable Frejus, you'll pull through well enough. You *have* to pull through, Zinn, because this town has a good deal to say that you ought to hear. Besides. . . ."

"Hell, man," said Peter Zinn, the savage, "I mean the dog. I mean Blondy. . . how. . . what I mean to say is . . ."

Then a great foreknowledge came upon Peter Zinn. His own life having been spared, fate had taken another in exchange, and Blondy would never lie warm upon his feet again. He closed his eyes and whispered huskily: "Say yes or no, Doc. Quick!"

But the doctor was in so little haste that he turned away and walked to the door, where he spoke in a low voice.

"He's got to have help," said Peter Zinn to his own dark heart. "He's got to have help to tell me how a growed-up man killed a poor pup."

Footsteps entered. "The real work I've been doing," said the doctor, "hasn't been with you. Look up, Zinn!"

Peter Zinn looked up, and over the edge of the doctor's arm he saw a long, narrow white head, with a pair of brown-black eyes and a wistfully wrinkled forehead. Blondy, swathed in soft white linen, was laid upon the bed and crept up closer until the cold point of his nose, after his fashion, was hidden in the palm of the master's hand. Now big Peter beheld the doctor through

197

a mist spangled with magnificent diamonds, and he saw that Burney found it necessary to turn his head away. He essayed speech which twice failed, but at the third effort he managed to say in a voice strange to himself: "Take it by and large, Doc, it's a damn' good old world."

# A FIRST BLOODING

*I am ending this collection with an excerpt from Faust's last attempt at major fiction. The title, "A First Blooding," is mine, and the story that follows has been fashioned, in parts, from an unfinished manuscript about the Civil War that Faust had called* **Wycherley***. This section of the novel was first printed in the 1990 Doubleday anthology,* **The New Frontier***, edited by Joe R. Lansdale, for which I wrote a special Afterword. In it, I stated: "By the 1940s, Faust had firmly established himself in the slick-paper markets. . . and had created the Dr. Kildare film series for M-G-M. (He wrote the first seven in the series.) Yet, with all this mass of popular wordage behind him, he had never published what he termed 'a really serious novel.' In 1940, he set himself the task of writing such a novel. . . . The War Between the States would form a crucible, a moral and physical testing ground, for the novel's protagonist, Allan Loring, a young officer serving with the Union Army." The book demanded extensive research; Faust's Civil War library eventually covered an entire wall of his study in Brentwood, California. The first fruit of this labor, a Civil War short story he called "A Watch and the Wilderness," was printed in* **Elk's Magazine** *in September of 1940; it was chosen by Faust for inclusion that same year in his first book of collected fiction,* **Wine on the Desert***. But the novel itself proved to be an extremely difficult task. For a writer capable of whipping out a Western novel in less than a week (and who had averaged two complete novels a month for many years), Faust's progress on* **Wycherley** *was*

199

*painfully slow. By early 1944, as he was ready to ship off for Italy to cover the war as a correspondent for* **Harper's**, *Faust had completed only a third of his projected novel—some 50,000 words. When he was killed by German mortar fire that May,* **Wycherley** *was put away and forgotten. Until the late 1980s, when Robert Easton, Faust's son-in-law, sent me a copy of the unfinished manuscript. From its two-hundred-and-nine typed pages I was able to extract this poignant action tale—a superb character study that ranks with his finest work, clear testimony to Frederick Faust's talent as a writer of "serious" prose.*

LIEUTENANT ALLAN LORING WAS BUILT AFTER THE true Yankee model, tall and heavy-boned, with the muscles fitted on hard and flat, like those of a mule. He moved toward the assembled patrol. The light from the open door of the guardhouse touched vaguely on shapeless uniforms and caps that sagged forward. The faces were dirty with new beards. Loring himself had tried to raise at least a pair of whiskers that might add dignity to his twenty-one years, but his mustaches grew in such irregular patches that he had to keep a clean skin.

Sergeant Means reported the detail ready, saluting with exaggerated precision.

Loring nodded, stepping smartly to the front of his patrol. In a moment he was striding at its head; the camp fell away behind him, and its odors of woodsmoke, coffee, and burned meat dissolved and left him alone in the night with the detail slogging steadily in his wake. As he walked, with nine men keeping the rhythm behind him, Loring felt there was a glorious purpose in the discipline of war that teaches men both to serve and to be masters. To his rapidly enlarging spirit there were no proper dimensions in the geography of earth, the blurred mist of woodlands, or the small undulation of the hills; he preferred to look up into the sky where the clouds were black mountains with the moon among them.

Here he struck up spray as high as his head by walking almost knee-deep into a puddle of rain water, and Loring became aware that, instead of a road, he was following random paths such as are bound to grow up near a camp. However, he had kept to a straight enough line, and yonder were the three tall trees which marked the outer limit of his patrol. The moon brightened them for an instant. He put his men in single file. In that formation they could make their way more readily through broken country. He noticed they were panting.

"The men seem a little blown, Sergeant," he said, proud of himself and his long legs.

"They are accustomed to the regulation step, sir," said the sergeant, after a moment of pause.

"Ah, and my step is too long?" asked Loring rather happily.

"By several inches, sir," said Means.

The soldiers looked darkly at their lieutenant, but still Loring felt very well about the matter as the march continued with the detail serpentining behind him through the brush. Usually, when he looked forward in his career, he found himself an officer beloved by his men, eventually scarred like an old mastiff but always considerately careful of the needs of his soldiers, in fact, a father to them, but, as he strode on again, it seemed to him that there was a less democratic ideal which might be of greater service to war and warriors, for are not soldiers better led by men above them? The very root of

201

the word "discipline" means docile willingness to learn from superiors.

Loring was resigning himself, now without pleasure, to this more Spartan conception when he heard the note of a night bird, flying low on the wind, so briefly uttered and so swiftly gone that he could not name it. He began to think of all the birds he had seen since he came to Virginia with the regiment—ruby-throated humming-birds, crested flycatchers, kingbirds, Baltimore and orchard orioles, bobolinks, indigo buntings, scarlet tanagers, rose-breasted grosbeaks, the vireos, warblers, Maryland yellowthroats, and above all the veery thrush. Only once had he seen its cinnamon-colored wings, but often in the woods he had heard the mysterious sound flowing from all sides, like light. It was only now and then, for moments, that one could even listen to the birds, for, as a rule, the mere thought of war was a deafening uproar in the mind.

At this, he roused himself from his thoughts to find that his long legs were carrying him through dense brush, so that in part he had been awakened by the soft cursing of the patrol which followed at his back. He was disturbed by something wrong in the scene before him, and he required a moment to discover what was missing: the moon had a clear moment in the sky, but nowhere could he find the three trees which were to be the limit of his march.

When he ventured a glance back and from side to side, he realized that he had lost his way utterly during those moments when he had been alone with his mind. Now, there was nothing for it except to admit to the sergeant that he was lost. The moonlight showed the chunky figure of Means, his fleshy brows slightly shadowed by a scowl as he grimly endured the folly of his superior.

The ground now sloped down toward a marshland where water glinted among the patches of brush and high grass. In fact, they had come close to the river, beyond which lay the South. A light wind carried the odor of mold and sun-cooked slime. The tall marsh grass in one place waved violently; a moment later a figure slipped out of the grass into a clump of shrubbery.

Loring halted his men with a raised hand. He pulled his revolver from its holster.

"Did you see, Sergeant?" he asked softly.

"Yes, sir," said Sergeant Means.

"Apt to be one of them trying to come through," said Loring. His own breath was short now, and not because of the distance he had tramped. He pointed, saying to his men: "Cover that patch of marsh grass with your guns. It's the big patch near the dead tree. . . where the bushes are moving. Something is coming through."

"A wild pig, maybe," said one of the men quietly.

Loring stood as though ready for target practice, with his left arm behind him and the gun held high, ready to be dropped on the mark. He had been very thorough in that part of his training, for, every time he handled the revolver, he could not help remembering that his skill with it might be life or death to him.

Except for himself and the sergeant, his command was on the ground, two kneeling, the others lying with their heavy muskets hugged to their shoulders, their heads twisted a bit to get the sights.

"Hold your breath when you aim," he remembered to tell them. "And don't shoot too high. Not too high, men!"

The wind was gone, so that the night had the familiar

sense of silence which is like fear itself. They were so close to the marsh that Loring could follow the small ripple, where a fish swam or a frog, across the oily silver of the moonlit water and even into the shadows. Wherever those shadows lay, whether beside the marsh grass, tree stumps, or derelict branches, the black of them was more real than the rest of the scene, like holes cut through a bright painting.

The furrow that plowed across the patch of brush now reached the edge of it, and a man appeared. From his slouched rag of a hat to his heels, he was so drenched that he looked more like a forked branch of a tree in motion than a human.

"Halt!" shouted Loring.

The figure whirled, leaping back into the bushes as Loring dropped the revolver on the mark. The sights came right on it, he thought, as he squeezed the trigger. The explosion boomed at his ear. The recoil jerked up the muzzle to readiness for the next shot, in perfect style, and then the muskets spat out little red snake-tongues of fire. The revolver had been like a terrier's bark; these were hounds in deep cry. The men were reloading, hurrying with their long ramrods, jamming the charges down the muzzles, while the smoke came bitter and sulphurous to the nostrils of Loring.

"Close in!" shouted Loring. "Close in!"

He began to run down the slope. He was slow on the level, but the pitch of the ground gave reach and drive to his striding. Even so, the sergeant got to the water before him, and Loring found himself thigh-deep, following. The ooze sucked at his ankles while man after man of his party got past him. He was panting as he dragged his weighted feet out of the slime onto the firm ground of the island. Breath came back to him

204

when he saw his men standing in a circle like hounds around a quarry. The fugitive, in the center of that trampled place, lay back on his elbows with his hand over a shoulder wound. Blood leaked through his fingers.

"Name of Barnet, Todd Barnet, Twenty-Seventh Virginia," reported the sergeant, who sat cross-legged, filling his pipe.

The wet slouch of a hat covered half the face of Barnet. A ten days' beard worked and bristled around his mouth as the pain put its teeth in him again and again. He had on shoes that looked homemade, and his attention seemed to be deeply fixed upon them. His trouser legs were worn to rags at the bottom. One shin, bared almost to the knee, was bone-white in the moonshine. "Turning up the toes" is a phrase for death; Loring thought of it as he stared at the Rebel, who was cursing Yankees and Yankee land as though sure of his privilege.

"You damn fools," he said. "What you still carrying pistols for? A musket ball would have clipped spang clean through me, but this here pistol ball it took and jarred off the bone and slipped down inside and murdered me."

The last of the detail came up, crunching the bushes underfoot, but, when they reached the place, they stood quietly. Some of them were masked by shadow, but the others looked the way Loring felt, very sick, for, like him, the new recruits were seeing their first death. He could remember a voice somewhere in his past talking about fox-hunting and "blooding the pack."

Barnet took a long breath, half vocal and quavering. Pain snapped shut his open mouth, and the sergeant looked curiously at him. There was no more sympathy in Means than in a small boy who has pulled a leg off a frog. The smoke from his pipe entered the still air in round little puffs of brightness, and the smell of it reminded Loring of the tutor who had solved for him the mystery of conditions in Greek verbs.

"That was a good shot, sir," said Means. "A very good shot."

The sickness was leaving the stomach and throat of Loring. The odor of the marsh had become to him the smell of death, but there was a new and more cruel manhood in him which was untroubled. Men must die in war.

"It's a damn' officer that done this to me, is it?" said the wounded man. "It's a dirty damn' Yank officer that knocked a hole in me?"

"Shut your mouth, Johnny," said the sergeant. He spoke sharply, as one gives command to a dog. He was protecting his own dignity as well as that of his commanding officer, but this sign of devotion enlarged the heart of Loring. He became a merciful conqueror.

"I know something about medicine," he said. "Let me look at the wound. I hope it won't be bad."

"You *hope*, do you?" asked the wounded man. "The hell you hope, you. . . ."

The words choked off in such a way that he thought Barnet was about to break down into sobbing; instead, he commenced to vomit. Two of the detail, hurrying off into the brush, imitated the prisoner, but Loring mastered his own nausea. He kneeled, tore up a handful of the long marsh grass, and wiped the muck from Barnet's face and throat.

The wounded man's eyes closed and opened again. He glared up at Loring. "You boys is gonna catch a whoppin' from us Rebs," he said. "We're gonna whop

206

you Yanks good an' proper." Then his eyes seemed to lose focus, and he began to speak as from a dream.

"We was in the lead of Jackson's column, and ole Stonewall was pulled up beside General Lee. It was the first time I'd ever seen Lee. His horse looked real small under him. . . that was my way of seein' that he was a big man.

"Stonewall had on that old cadet's cap, and he was all covered with dust and suckin' on a lemon. He had the visor of the cap drawn way down because the dust burned his eyes to bits, you know.

"It was getting late, an' the woods was sort of smudging together, and that seemed to let the Yanks get up close to us. A lot of our boys was passin' to the rear, wounded. A lot more lay here and there, as tired as dying. They'd get up and flop down and drag up again. Some of them wounded was pretty bad.

"A. P. Hill was up there on the ridge holdin' on, but he was bein' wore down. We went along toward the trouble in a double line with orders to trail arms and do no shootin' till the word came. A fellow beside me said . . . 'That means we're gonna charge.'"

Barnet's face was chalky, his breathing heavy and labored, but the words kept flowing.

"General Hood, he brought us up on the left of Law, and it seems that he saw a gap and open country in between Law and Pickett. He ordered us into that hole, and we went on the double through Hill's men. They didn't get up and join the charge. They just lay squashed into the ground and watched us go by. That's how much they'd been through. It was as though every one of them had been bled white. We come up over the ridge. Down below us was the marsh. Going downhill was easier for our legs. But the boys was droppin' pretty fast. You

207

know how they fall sometimes, curling up small? It seemed to me that half of our boys went down like that, shot right through the guts. I thought I was up toward the front, but somebody had been there before me. I remember him sittin' up and yellin' for water, water. . . there was too much noise to hear his voice, but his mouth was sayin'. . . 'Water! Water'. . . and opening wide, like a frog. I didn't stop. . . but every step, I felt as though I was gonna die.

"We was close up under the Yanks, and then all at once we was in among them. I pushed a bayonet at one of 'em. He tied himself up in a knot around my gun. I kept pushin', but the bayonet was stuck, and I couldn't pull it out till I fired into his belly. And when I'd reloaded, the Yanks was on the run everywhere. We went after 'em through the swamp with our legs mighty tired, but our boys was half crazy because we knew we'd cut through the worst of the trouble. Pretty soon, we could hear yelling, left and right, and then we was gobblin' up prisoners till there didn't seem to be any Yanks left. Well, that's about all. Guess it don't amount to much. Mostly beginning and not much end."

The wind began to rise, and it blew the sweating face of Loring as cold as the marsh slime. Barnet, with every outward breath, was groaning.

"We're gonna whop you." It was hard to understand him now, for the loose slobber of his lips could not frame the words, and he seemed to breathe them forth without articulation. "Us Rebs is goin' to whop you."

Loring's left hand and sleeve were foul with blood. Behind him he heard the quiet voice of the sergeant saying: "It's his first one. He's got to make the most of him." Then: "This here's a fine place to catch the marsh fever. Day's not so bad as night. The air's thicker at

208

night. It lets the rot into you."

Todd Barnet was staring up at Loring. "You kin do a favor for me, Yank."

"And what's that?" asked Loring.

"You kin give me a drink. . . a wee swaller. Will you do that?" And he slipped from his elbows and lay flat.

"Canteen," directed Loring.

"He don't need it," said the sergeant.

Loring looked down at Todd Barnet.

"He's done," declared Means.

The body of Barnet, diminished by death, seemed to be sinking into the marshy ground.

"We ought to do something," said Loring. "We ought to bury the body."

"Nothin' to bury him in," said Means. "Just the damn' marsh."

On their right, two men were advancing down the slope, one a pace to the rear of the other as though attending someone of importance. An Army major, and yet his insignia of rank was so lost under the cloak he wore that he seemed more like a country gentleman who had chosen an odd hour for walking abroad. He was a large man, and, as he moved, his long cloak swaggered from side to side. When Loring saluted, he answered with a wave of his hand which had nothing military about it. He stopped beside the body of Barnet and lit a cigar.

"Hello, Lieutenant!"

"Sir," said Loring.

"Did you do this?"

"Yes, sir."

"What's your name, son?"

"Loring, sir. Ninety-Second Massachusetts."

"I'm Major Acton." He turned the cigar slowly in his

mouth. "This your first dead man?"

"Yes, sir."

"I'll need a report."

"Yes, sir."

Ⓥ Ⓥ Ⓥ Ⓥ Ⓥ

Major Acton lived in a cabin no better than any pair of soldiers in the Army of the Potomac might have constructed for their winter quarters. It was walled with logs chinked with mud and straw, and a tent made the roof; he had an Indian bed of springy willow, a fireplace, a table, stools, and a door made of hardtack boxes. There was not even a floor, which many a private soldier was at pains to build for himself, and the only distinguishing features of his furniture were the shelves of books, closely packed, above his fireplace, and a closet that, when opened, offered a shining, thick display of bottles and cigar boxes. Four of the latter, empty, supported candles which were fixed in their own drippings. It was a dank, uncomfortable shanty. The wet clothes of Loring, as he sat at the table bent above his report, clung to his shanks and gave him a cold promise of chills and fever.

When his head grew heavy in the beginning, he had refreshed himself with a taste of the whiskey that the major put beside him, but he was not familiar with the stuff, and it made him slightly ill. He could see that the major constantly was sipping from a tall glass, tilting a bottle now and then to replenish his supply, but the eye of Acton never grew bleared. Loring thought of the gossip that the Army contained officers who were true two-bottle men: one for health and one for pleasure, as the saying went.

A knock at the door. The major called out, and a sergeant entered the cabin, followed by three privates, two of them obviously keeping guard over the third, who was unarmed.

The sergeant saluted. He reported that the prisoner, picked up behind the lines, straggling, had claimed to belong to the Fifteenth New Jersey. He gave the name of Christopher Hodge, but Colonel Collet carried no such name on the rolls of his regiment.

"Well, Hodge?" asked Major Acton. "Are you a New Jersey man?"

The prisoner scratched his head, screwed up his face comically, and winked.

"Nary hide nor hair," he said.

He was a tall young man, lean of flesh and large of bone. The layered tan of his face was weathered like old oak.

"Where are you at home?" asked the major.

"It kind of depends," said Hodge. "But mostly don't folks say that home is where your ma and pappy was born and raised?"

"Yes, usually," said the major. "And where *were* your mother and father raised?"

"Clean up to Vermont," said Hodge.

"That's pretty far north," agreed the major. "Where were you born?"

"The same, sir, sure enough. But they took and moved me down to Louisiana."

"Pleasant place, I'm told," said the major in the kindest of voices.

"Mighty pleasant some ways," said Hodge. "They got pretty fences down there at Louisiana, all Cherokee roses and sweetbrier, so's you can't find the rails of the fences inside the thicket, and the trumpet creepers and

211

the grapevines and even cane grows right up through the roses, so's every foot of the way down a road is different from every other foot."

"Rich land, isn't it?" asked the major, growing more and more neighborly.

"It's fine and rich in the hollows and the flats, mostly," said Hodge, "but you can see young pines on the high places, and where the pines come, it's sure that soil has washed thin. But it's good earth."

"That's a hard country to leave," said the major.

"It is and it ain't," said Hodge.

Loring began to look more closely at Hodge and gather words with which to paint him in letters, knowing that this was a scene to be remembered, to be kept in hand when, after the storm, he found himself once again ashore among the long, quiet days of peace. He had felt at first that the major was examining the man, drawing him out, that he might at last make a false step, but now Acton seemed to drift into an attitude of acceptance, genially nodding agreement even before Hodge answered a question. This journey of one man among enemies through half the scope of the continent gave to Loring's imagination the material out of which he already was building a whole odyssey.

"It's a long journey, Hodge," said the major.

"It ain't so short as to the schoolhouse," agreed Hodge, "but I got me a job teaming for the Army, and I kept shifting north and farther north. Took me six whole months to get here. I been cussin' mules in Louisianan and Mississippian and Alabaman and Georgian, and I've had to take and fight some Carolina mules, too, and they was the orneriest of the lot."

"So finally you wound up on the right side?"

"I sure did," said Hodge, his face growing bright. "I

thought it was going to be pretty hard to get through the lines, but it wasn't so. I just kept walkin' till I seen some of the boys takin' a swim in a creek, and I heard them talkin', their voices comin' with an echo up from the water, and they talked Fifteenth New Jersey. So I just took and borrowed some of their clothes. I didn't borrow no whole man's outfit, but I lifted a coat here and a pair of pants there, till I fixed myself up and didn't make nobody go naked. And so, then I just walked on until finally I was stopped and asked questions, and they brought me here."

"Why did you take the uniform at all?" asked the major. "Why not simply tell them that you were a friend coming over to the right side?"

"I ain't one of the bright ones," said Hodge, "but then I ain't simple, neither. If you try to come over without no uniform, they take and shoot you first and ask you questions afterward."

"What will you do in Vermont?" asked Acton.

"Farm work, 'most any kind, sir," said Hodge.

"You've been used to that, eh?"

"Yes, sir. I can plow or reap or thrash or mostly anything on a farm, I guess."

"You're a brave, cool fellow, Hodge," said the major. "And the clothes you have on *used* to be the uniform of the Fifteenth New Jersey."

Hodge grew slowly taller. To the anxious eye of Loring he did not seem to change color, but the words of the major had straightened him, taking the slouch out of his back.

"Your friends have done a very poor job for you, Mister Hodge," said the major. "They must have heard that this Army is now composed of corps which use badges. The Fifteenth New Jersey is in the Sixth Corps,

213

Mister Hodge, and, if you had stolen a uniform from one of them, you would have found on it a cross. . . the cross in the First Division is red."

Hodge laughed. "That's what there was on the coat," he said. "And I took and tore it off, because I was afeared it might mean something special, like a medal for service, and I ain't nothing special, sir. Just a Louisiana farmer is all. I didn't want no hard questions put to me, because I right well couldn't've answered them."

Acton was shaking his head slowly, as though he were reluctant to disagree.

"If you'd torn off the cross, it would have left a mark on the cloth."

However mild his voice, he was calling Hodge a liar. The air which Loring breathed had a different taste. It sickened him. Hodge was trying to laugh again, but it was no good this time, for, behind the laughter, his eyes were wandering in a desperate mist. He was like an actor alone in the center of the stage with his lines forgotten.

"It's no good, old fellow, is it?" asked the major.

The laughter of Hodge stopped. It hushed suddenly, leaving his face distorted. After a moment he was able to say: "No, I suppose it's no good."

"Pour him a drink, Loring," said the major, "and have another yourself."

From the first, Loring now realized, Acton had seen through the spy but had not wished to cut the scene short, instead, he had been lingering out his enjoyment. The soldiers of the guard had come in like hunters with a trophy, their pleasure gradually fading as the major's friendly conversation was prolonged, but now they were keen again, handling their muskets and taking a new

214

grip with their eyes on this quarry that had almost escaped.

Loring poured some whiskey and offered it to Hodge, the liquid shuddering in the glass. "I'm sorry," he said.

The shock had brought out a fine sweat on Hodge. Perhaps this was the true agony and all that followed would be easy.

"You're a kind fellow," he said as he took the whiskey.

Loring watched the glass steady in the hand of Hodge. He felt relief like an intake of breath, for he saw that the man intended to die well.

"Well, here's health to everyone," said Hodge, raising the glass to them. And he drained it. "Ah, that's good stuff," he said, and seemed surprised that chance had placed such excellent whiskey in Yankee hands.

"Get that sort of goods in Carolina?" asked Acton.

"You had me spotted all the time?" said Hodge. Being about to die, he, nevertheless, was embarrassed that his deception had been so easily penetrated.

"No, that was mostly guessing," admitted the major. "It was the lack of the badge that hurt you."

"That's *their* fault, not mine," said Hodge.

"Entirely," agreed the major. "Will you have another taste of whiskey?"

"Another? No, no! That one took the chill out," said Hodge.

"It's necessary for me to tell you," said Acton, "that, if you'll give us the information you have at hand, everything can be arranged for you."

"Information?" repeated Hodge, then his ugly face flushed. "I haven't any information."

"Of course not," said the major, "but we have to make the proposal."

It seemed to Loring that there was a hint of apology from Major Acton.

"I'm ready now, Major," said Hodge.

Acton shook hands with him.

"They should have given you the right uniform," he said. "They really should." And he nodded to the sergeant.

"Atten-SHUN!" said the sergeant quietly.

His men fell in beside the prisoner.

"Good bye, Mister Hodge." The major saluted, and the party disappeared through the door.

"Does he *have* to die?" asked Loring.

"Naturally," answered the major.

He canted his head a little to one side, listening, sipping his drink rather furtively. Then someone shouted. Two or three guns exploded, and there was a yell of satisfaction.

"Ah, yes," said the major, smiling and nodding. "*That* was a rare fellow."

Ⓥ Ⓥ Ⓥ Ⓥ Ⓥ

The outer night, in which Christopher Hodge had just died, was as black as a tar barrel with a faint streak of brightness at the top of it, as though the barrel were slanted toward the polar star.

Loring found his cabin and went into it as noiselessly as possible; nevertheless, he blundered before he got his clothes off, and Watrous cleared his throat with distinctness to let it be known that he'd been wakened. The need for talk ached in the throat of Loring, but he knew it would be foolish to speak. He lay in his blankets on his back and stared up at the ray of a star that managed to slide through a crevice in the roof. His breath grew a bit short from pressure across his shoulder blades, but, when he turned on his side, he inclined his head downward and sank his thoughts into a thicker gloom.

All the distances and dates of his existence had altered. From Massachusetts to the Rapidan had seemed a great journey, and from childhood to the present had been a monstrous stretch of time, but now all the years could be put into the balance against the hours of this single day. He saw with the mind's eye, by that Homeric light which casts no shadow, what war would always mean to him.

Somewhere a detail was marching through a rhythmical sloshing of mud. The detail turned an invisible corner into silence. In a cabin nearby, a man moved in his bunk with a creak of boards, but again the silence fitted down quickly and closely, like a black woolen cap drawn over the ears.

And, at last, Loring slept.

THE END

# About the Author

**Max Brand** is the best-known pen name of Frederick Faust, creator of Dr. Kildare, Destry, and many other fictional characters popular with readers and viewers worldwide. Faust wrote for a variety of audiences in many genres. His enormous output, totaling approximately thirty million words or the equivalent of 530 ordinary books, covered nearly every field: crime, fantasy, historical romance, espionage, Westerns, science fiction, adventure, animal stories, love, war, and fashionable society, big business and big medicine. Eighty motion pictures have been based on his work along with many radio and television programs. For good measure he also published four volumes of poetry. Perhaps no other author has reached more people in more different ways.

Born in Seattle in 1892, orphaned early, Faust grew up in the rural San Joaquin Valley of California. At Berkeley he became a student rebel and one-man literary movement, contributing prodigiously to all campus publications. Denied a degree because of unconventional conduct, he embarked on a series of adventures culminating in New York City where, after a period of near starvation, he received simultaneous recognition as a serious poet and successful author of fiction. Later, he traveled widely, making his home in New York, then in Florence, and finally in Los Angeles.

Once the United States entered the Second World War, Faust abandoned his lucrative writing career and his work as a screenwriter to serve as a war correspondent with the infantry in Italy, despite his fifty-one years and a bad heart. He was killed during a night attack on a hilltop village held by the German army. New books based on magazine serials or unpublished manuscripts or restored versions continue to appear so that, alive or dead, he has averaged a new book every four months for seventy-five years. Beyond this, some work by him is newly reprinted every week of every year in one or another format somewhere in the world. A great deal more about this author and his work can be found in *The Max Brand Companion* (Greenwood Press, 1997) edited by Jon Tuska and Vicki Piekarski.

We hope that you enjoyed reading this
Sagebrush Large Print Western.
If you would like to read more Sagebrush titles,
ask your librarian or contact the Publishers:

## United States and Canada

Thomas T. Beeler, *Publisher*
Post Office Box 659
Hampton Falls, New Hampshire 03844-0659
(800) 251-8726

## United Kingdom, Eire, and
## the Republic of South Africa

Isis Publishing Ltd
7 Centremead
Osney Mead
Oxford OX2 0ES  England
(01865) 250333

## Australia and New Zealand

Australian Large Print Audio & Video P/L
17 Mohr Street
Tullamarine, Victoria, 3043, Australia
1 800 335 364